KU-090-414

XB00 000017 9353

Black Gold

After being paid off for delivering horses to the army, Del Gannon and his partner, Johnny Concho, stop off in Yuma. Del aims to quit the tough business of bronc busting and buy an orange farm in California. Johnny holds the money while Del gets cleaned up in readiness for signing the contract, but Johnny is robbed and killed.

Bent on revenge, Del finds the killers and rescues a young Indian, Lone Wolf, from their clutches, but one of the killers escapes. Lone Wolf, the son of Yuma Indian chief, Painted Tail, presents Del with some mysterious black stones.

The part these stones play in bringing Johnny's killer to justice makes for a breath-taking scenario in a tale of duplicity and courage.

By the same author

High Plains Vendetta
Dance with the Devil
Nugget!
Montezuma's Legacy
Death Rides Alone
Gambler's Dawn
Vengeance at Bittersweet
Justice for Crockett
Bluecoat Renegade
Gunsmoke over New Mexico
Montaine's Revenge

Writing as Ethan Flagg

Dead Man Walking
Two for Texas
Divided Loyalties
Return of the Gunfighter
Dynamite Daze
Apache Rifles
Duel at Del Norte
Outlaw Queen
When Lightning Strikes
Praise be to Silver
A Necktie for Gifford

Black Gold

Dale Graham

ROBERT HALE · LONDON

First published in Great Britain 2013

ISBN 978-0-7198-0594-3

Robert Hale Limited
Clerkenwell House
Clerkenwell Green
London EC1R 0HT

www.halebooks.com

Typeset by
Derek Doyle & Associates, Shaw Heath
Printed and bound in Great Britain by
CPI Antony Rowe, Chippenham and Eastbourne

ONE

PAY-OFF

'Hey, Del! How yuh gonna spend your wages?'

The ebullient shout came from a young guy on the far side of the string of mustangs. Johnny Concho's high-spirited enquiry was aimed at a tall, raw-boned rider who exhibited a detached yet reflective demeanour as he considered the enquiry. Despite their different characters, the pair of bronc-busters had become firm buddies during their three months of breaking wild horses in the wilderness of southern Arizona's Eagletail Mountains.

Del Gannon threw a laconic smile at his partner. The kid's wild and untamed nature would sure benefit from some busting of its own. He eyed the young puncher with a measured and thoughtful regard. The older laid-back Texan felt a certain paternal responsibility towards his young associate.

'Well?' urged the excited buster. 'We gonna have a

blast in Yuma once the boss has paid us off?'

'Maybe a couple of drinks to clear this dust outa my throat,' agreed Gannon slowly, 'but the rest is going into the bank.'

'You got plans, Del?' The remark came from bossman Jake Bundy.

'Figured on saving up to buy my own spread in California,' replied the tall Texan while rolling a cigarette one-handed.

'You ain't goin' into competition with me, are yuh?'

Del laughed. 'Oranges, Jake. Oranges.' Bundy gave the comment a puzzled frown. His compadre waved a brochure in his face. 'There's a place up for sale in California's San Joaquin Valley. Reckon I'm going to put in a bid when we get to Yuma.'

'Never figured you for a sodbuster, Del,' remarked Bundy scratching his bald head.

'Age catches up with us all, Jake. Busting wild broncs is a young man's game. And I'm getting too long in the tooth.' The parting comment drifted on the low breeze as Del Gannon spurred his mount towards the front of the herd.

The outfit, which comprised of five busters including Del Gannon and his young buddy were drawing close to Bender's Fort. The herd amounted to a little over a hundred horses that had been specially peeled for use by the cavalry.

It had been a tough three months working non-stop from dawn 'til dusk. A punishing routine that resulted in no bronc-peeler escaping without injury.

But these guys were as tough and hardy as the wild horses they trained. Luckily, none of the maulings had been of an overly serious nature, just the usual bruises and sprains.

In truth, Gannon, like the rest of the boys, was ready for a break and some well-earned rest and relaxation. Not that there would be much of that once they hit the nearest town.

Jake Bundy was a strict but fair employer. He had insisted on running an alcohol-free outfit to ensure his men kept to their task. As a result, the boys were more than ready to hit the flesh pots of Yuma, which was also the home of the infamous Arizona State Penitentiary.

It was another two hours of chewing dust before the starkly brutal structure hove into view.

All eyes swung towards this grim bastion of law enforcement as they passed by a quarter-mile to the north. Only the steady plod of trotting horses disturbed the ether. Of birds, there was none to be seen. Indeed all creatures appeared to have given the prison a wide berth.

At that precise moment a bell commenced tolling inside the thick walls.

'What's that?' asked Jess Norton, nudging his brother Frank.

It was Del Gannon who provided the answer. 'They always toll the bell before a hanging,' he said quietly.

Sharp intakes of breath followed the grim announcement. Only when they had passed the austere premises did the mood lighten. It was as if they had all been holding their breath. Such was the macabre reputation of Yuma Prison.

'Boy, I sure don't wanna end up in that berg,' gasped Concho, drawing a grubby bandanna across his sweating brow.

The others earnestly nodded their agreement.

The small township of Yuma lay in a shallow depression at the bottom of a three-mile long grade with Bender's Fort another five miles to the west.

Arriving at the eastern edge of Yuma, they all paused. A notice was affixed to the post beneath where the town's name was daubed in green paint.

It read: *No horses, steers, pigs, sheep or other critters to be driven down the main street. Failure to comply is a serious offence.* And it was signed: *Clu Taggart, Town Marshal.*

'What say we give old Clu a surprise?' hooted Concho with glee. 'We can be out the other side afore he knows what's happened.'

Bundy shook his head, his grey eyes raised to the heavens as he gave the suggestion a terse response.

'Weren't it you, kid, that said he didn't fancy a spell in the pen?'

The blood drained from the young tearaway's face.

'They wouldn't.' He gaped open-mouthed from Bundy across to his partner. 'Would they, Del?'

'You want to find out, Conch?'

'Guess not,' came the subdued response. And so the string of horses was channeled around the outer fringes of the town.

Once the men had been paid, they wished each other well and headed off in different directions. The Norton brothers, Jess and Frank, had never been to Mexico. And, as the border was only a half-day's ride to the south, they decided against returning to Yuma. A couple of drinks in the fort saloon and they were ready to ride.

The boss intended riding with them as far as San Luis where he had heard tell there were ready-broke horses for sale.

'Guess I won't be seeing you again next spring. That right, Del?' The head wrangler was still hoping that his associate would change his mind about becoming a farmer. 'This was our third year working together. And there ain't no doubt about it: Del Gannon is the best durned bronc-peeler I ever had on the team.'

Bundy waited expectantly, hoping.

'Reckon not, Jake,' mused the Texan. 'My mind's made up. Another season of being kicked about from pillar to post will see me into an early grave. I've got my sights set on making a go of that farm.'

'Well now,' smiled Bundy repeating his previous barbed comment, 'never figured you for a nester. Thought hoss breakin' was in your blood.'

Del shrugged. 'I seen too many guys get crippled from not knowing when to stop. That ain't for me.'

'Well, good luck to you.' Bundy accorded his old partner a doleful shrug, then held out a hand which Del accepted. 'If'n you ever change your mind, you know where to find me.'

A brief nod and Bundy left to follow in the wake of the Norton boys.

Only Del and his young sidekick returned to Yuma.

TWO

BUSTED!

Being a border town, Yuma attracted a host of itinerant traders from both sides of the line. And mixed in were an equal measure of bandits and owlhoots fleeing from US and Mexican law-enforcement agencies. The very fact that Yuma was home to the notorious prison made little difference: it only served to make these denizens of the underworld more disdainful of authority.

Knowing they could quickly escape over the border into Mexico imbued in them a reckless bravado. It was a brave man indeed who accepted the job of starpacker in such a den of iniquity. Clu Taggart was just such a man. Since his arrival the town had quietened down some.

Del nudged his faithful chestnut mare down the main street with Johnny Concho by his side. The kid was all eyes. He was eager for some fun.

Leaning towards a vacant hitching rail, they both dismounted and tied off. Del shook the stiffness from his ageing muscles. After removing the saddle-bag containing both his and Johnny's pay, he signalled the kid over.

'Reckon I can trust you, boy?' he asked, instilling a serious tone into the question.

'Sure yuh can, Del. You know that.' The kid was somewhat piqued to have his reliablity doubted. 'Why yuh askin' such a danged fool question? We're partners, ain't we?'

'That's cos I have a very important job for you.' Gannon lowered his voice, peering about to ensure their conversation was not being overheard. 'I need to get a haircut and bath real bad before I visit the land agent who's after selling that orange farm in the San Joaquin Valley.'

Johnny sniffed. 'You don't smell so bad to me.' he opined.

'That might be cos you're no better. We both need a good scrubdown. But you can have your'n later. This business is more important.' He handed over the heavy leather bag. 'You keep a hold of this while I'm in the tub. And guard it real close. That's our whole future in there.'

Johnny clutched the bag to his chest.

'You can depend on me, Del,' he replied with exagerated gravity. 'I'll guard it with my life.'

Del responded with a curt nod. 'We'll meet back here in one hour. While I'm gone, you go sit in that café over yonder.' He pointed across the street to a red and white painted clapboard structure bearing the singular legend: *Maggy May's Magic Munch House – A mouthwatering experience.* 'And don't move out of there until I get back.'

'You got my word on that, Del,' Johnny assured his buddy staunchly.

Del then dug into the bag and handed over a five dollar bill. 'Get yourself the biggest steak they serve with all the trimmings.'

'Gee thanks,' breezed the kid. 'It's got me slaverin' like a hound dog just to think on it.'

The two busters parted company. Del headed off down the street towards a Chinese bath-house he had spotted. Concho just stood there, looking about him open-mouthed. He was still in awe at being in such a notorious town.

As he made to cross the street, a group of cowpokes came bustling out of a saloon just a block down. Jinglebobs on their spurs trilled merrily as they stamped along the boardwalk.

From inside the saloon, the lilting cadence of a showgirl's voice drifted through the open door. It was accompanied by the spirited backing of a small house band. Johnny suddenly realized what he had been missing all these months shut away in the bleak wilderness of the Eagletails.

He hesitated, torn between his promise to Del Gannon and the need for some fun. It was a tough decision. The kid had no wish to go against his partner's ruling. But just one drink, and one song? Surely Del wouldn't grudge him that. Then he'd go have that meal.

His conscience appeased, Johnny Concho quickly hustled down the sidewalk and into the Border Post Saloon.

A wall of discordant bellowing assaulted the kid's ears. The patrons were accompanying the singer who was cavorting on a stage at the far end of the room. Meant to be a tuneful rendition of '*Get along little dogies*', it was more akin to the howling of a thousand tortured banshees. And Johnny loved it. Men were dancing in the central area to a four-piece band, half of them with each other.

Women appeared to be in short supply.

Johnny weaved a course through the swaying throng across to the bar.

'What'll it be, stranger?' shouted a barman, his voice straining to penetrate the raucous din.

The kid merely pointed to one of the beer taps. The guy nodded and pulled the drink.

Unthinking, Johnny unfastened the straps of his saddle-bags and fished out a handful of bills pushing one across to the barkeep.

'And give me a couple of them cigars,' he added.

The guy complied, then frowned at the proffered note. Scooping up the twenty, he studied it with a practised eye. It wasn't often he saw large denomination banknotes like this. The bill appeared genuine so he stuck it in his pocket and doled out the change.

Johnny pushed a fiver back across the bar. 'Have one yourself,' he breezed, taking a large gulp of his drink.

'Much obliged. Mind if'n I have it later?' replied the 'keep pocketing the note. All tips went that way. It helped boost his wages. Johnny shrugged off the query. 'You from around these parts?' continued the barman eager to retain this well-heeled customer.

Johnny emptied the pot before replying. Smacking his lips, he pushed the glass back across the bar for a refill. That drink had barely touched his throat. Another was needed to savour at his leisure.

'Me and my buddies have just finished busting a pile of wild mustangs up in the Eagletails. We just got paid off.' He took a swig from the refilled glass. 'I sure needed that,' he gasped. 'My throat felt like a dried-up river-bed.'

'You staying in Yuma long?'

'Naw!' Johnny swayed. After such a long spell on the wagon, he was unused to the effects of the demon drink. 'First thing in the morning, me and my partner are headin' fer California to buy a place of our own.'

The frenetic clamour in the Border Post failed to hide the brief exchange.

Three men along the bar had witnessed the unintentional display from Johnny Concho. And their interest was piqued. Hunched over their drinks, the shady trio were always on the lookout for easy pickings that could be purloined from gullible jackasses.

Cabel Sharkey was the leader. A hard-boiled jasper, his flickering gaze was made all the more sinister by a knife scar that had given him a permanent scowl.

Gingerly he sidled closer. Nudging the heavy-set bruiser on his right, he gestured for him to take heed of the overt show being given by the greenhorn kid.

Mad Dog Regan's eyes bulged. If the kid was paying for a drink with such a large note, there must be a heap more in that bag. A gnarled hand caressed the large Bowie knife strapped to his belt as a knowing look passed between the two gunslingers.

The third member of the gang was a tall, lanky jasper whose cadaverous features had given him the natural appendage of Reaper. Nobody knew his real name. And Reaper had never bothered to acquaint them. One look at the waxen skull precluded any such enquiries.

'This punk is just invitin' some enterprisin' jiggers to help themselves,' he whispered to his sidekicks. The remark was laced with macabre intent. Evil smiles devoid of humour concurred with the suggestion.

'And that's gonna be us, boys,' replied Sharkey, finishing his drink. Levering himself off the bar the gang boss signalled for the others to follow him outside. Once on the boardwalk, Sharkey outlined his plan to relieve Johnny Concho of his and his partner's hard-earned dough.

They didn't have long to wait.

It was another quarter-hour before the kid emerged from the saloon. He belched loudly swaying, a mite unsteady on his feet.

A dusky mantle was already settling across the town as the waning light of day faded. Lengthening shadows crept silently across the street, their remorseless advance creating dark enclaves ideal for snaring the unawary.

Johnny turned to make his way down the street. His gaze was fixed on Maggy May's diner over on the far side. At that time, there were few people abroad. Shops had closed and most respectable folks were indoors.

A cat squealed beneath the boards doubtless having just secured its own mousy supper.

While passing the first entry between the saloon and a dry goods store, Johnny was attracted by what appeared to be a fearful call for assistance.

'Help, somebody help me!'

The whining plea came from behind the frontages of the main street premises. Johnny paused, arrowing a narrowed look down the alley. A few scuffles and bumps were followed by another appeal for help.

'Ain't nobody out there gonna help me?' The entreaty was cut short by a brutal thump. 'Aaaaagh!'

That was enough for Johnny Concho. Gritting his teeth, the kid made to enter the darkened portal of the alley. But he could see nothing. Everything was a blur of umbrid shadows. Considering himself a plucky dude not lacking courage or nerve, he girded his loins and plunged headlong into the gloom of the alleyway.

Emerging at the rear he was met by a semi-circle of three men, none of whom appeared to be in any sort of danger.

'What's this all about?' he queried.

'Get him!' growled the larger of the trio. 'And no guns. We don't want to alert the town.'

Instantly the other two moved into action.

Caught wrong-footed and somewhat the worse for his recent noggins, Johnny was stunned by a straight left connecting with his jaw.

He staggered back as the second man came at him. A swinging haymaker from Mad Dog Regan sought out the kid's head. Had it connected, that would have decisively terminated the one-sided contest. Luckily the kid saw it coming and slewed to one side at the last moment. The ham-like fist whistled by throwing Regan off balance.

But Johnny Concho was no milksop. If it had done nothing else, busting wild horses had certainly toughened him up. Without thought he swung the heavy saddle-bag at Regan's bullet of a head. The heavy thud brought a smile of satisfaction to the kid's face as the hardcase fell to his knees. He then threw the bag at the tall beanpole who had thrown the first punch.

Reaper easily brushed it aside.

He dived at Johnny wrestling him to the ground. Over and over they rolled, each trying to land a punishing blow. But the kid's superior strength won out. Finding himself on top of the corpse-like figure, he jabbed a left then a right at the angular skull, busting the critter's nose. Blood pumped from the mashed proboscis. Reaper desperately scuttled out of reach on all fours.

Johnny leapt to his feet crouching low ready for

the next attack. He was given no time to draw breath as Cabel Sharkey joined the fray. The mean-eyed *hombre* threw a meaty right which Johnny blocked, retaliating with a hard jab to his assailant's midriff. Sharkey doubled over, a whoosh of air escaping from his open mouth.

The ambush was not going the way he had planned. This guy was not the pushover he had expected. Sharkey backed off as Johnny came at him. But three against one were not good odds. He had forgotten about Mad Dog Regan who had unknowingly gotten behind him.

The Dog had not acquired his bestial monicker by attending Sunday school picnics. An ugly snarl hissed from between clenched teeth as he grabbed the hilt of the large knife. Stepping up cat-like behind the wild-eyed kid, he drove it hard into his back until it would go no further.

Such was the rabid force behind the stabbing that the point of the blade emerged from the front of the kid's shirt. Blood oozed from the deadly cut. A tight gasp issued from Johnny's pinched features. Back arching with shock, he threw back his arms, legs weakening from the fatal strike. Tottering forward a couple more steps, he dropped to his knees and keeled over.

The killers just stood over the dead body, unmoving.

Harsh clasps of breath, more from pent-up tension than the brutal assault had concussed their brains. It was Sharkey who recovered first. This had been much tougher than any of them had bargained on. He grabbed up the saddle-bags.

'Check that the bastard's dead,' he snapped, while peering up the alley. Nobody appeared to have heard the fracas. The blunt order quickly brought the other two round.

Reaper toed the still body over on to its back and bent down for a closer look. 'An undertaker is all this jasper needs,' he declared, standing up.

'Then let's get outa here pronto,' ordered Sharkey while quickly frisking the corpse for anything else of value. A half smile broke over cracked features when he found a gold pocket watch. The item disappeared into his pocket. 'Afore some nosy varmint comes by and trips over him.'

The other two didn't need any second bidding. All three of the bushwackers disappeared into the gloom. Moments later, the pounding of hoofs broke the silence of early evening. That soon faded to nought as the killers made good their escape.

Only the haunting melody of a night owl broke the stillness. A mournful requiem to the swift and brutal exit of Johnny Concho.

THREE

PIT OF DESPAIR

Del felt like a new man. He looked it too.

A bath and haircut later, he was clad in new duds, his hair slicked back with pomade and smelling like a tart's boudoir. A broad smile creased the tanned visage. Following the removal of all that muck and fuzz, he was now clearly visible as a ruggedly handsome dude.

He smiled to himself. Not even Jake Bundy would recognize him.

And not only that: he had just agreed to buy the orange farm that his heart had been set upon. All that was required now was the signing of the contract along with the registration of the fifty per cent deposit.

The crafty land agent had tried to wheedle the full amount from him but Del was having none of it.

'Half up front and half when I've viewed the property and can see that it's a going concern.' he argued forcefully.

'It is the normal business practice of this agency to collect the full amount when the contract is signed,' preened the pompous dude, his nose twitching with irritation.

Del fastened a piercing blue eye on to the unctuous weasel.

'You wouldn't buy a horse from me without seeing it and having a ride,' he purred, 'and making certain it ain't some flea-bitten old nag, would you?'

The agent huffed but was forced to concede the point. 'Guess not.'

'Well neither would I.' He held out his hand. 'Do we have a deal?'

The twittering agent hesitated. He could refuse and wait for another buyer. But that farm had been up for sale now this past two months. And time is money. If this guy was willing to pay the full asking price, then why not agree to his terms? 'OK, it's a deal,' he said somewhat diffidently.

So here Del was about to have his dreams become reality.

Starlight twinkling overhead complemented a bouyant mood as the ex-bronc buster entered Maggie May's diner. He paused inside the door. Bright eyes panned the interior searching out his young partner.

That was when the smile began to slip.

Where was the kid?

Maybe he'd just slipped out back to relieve himself. For a second time, concerned eyes probed the seated diners.

'Can I help you, sir?'

Del quickly scanned the eating-house again just in case he'd missed spotting Johnny. Nothing. A dark frown ribbed his forehead.

'Has a young fella been in here wearing buckskins and a black hat with silver conchos?'

'I've been here since noon and nobody of that description has been served by me.' The waitress turned to address another girl. She repeated the description, but the other girl shook her head. 'Sorry, sir. Would you be wanting a table yourself. Maybe your friend has been delayed.'

Del ignored the question. Yeah he mused. The young hothead had been delayed all right – in the nearest saloon. His mood soured even more. Wait 'til I get hold of that pesky varmint.

He was accorded no further chance to mull over the dire consequences that would befall his wayward partner. A harsh yell outside drew his attention.

'Get the marshal!' The hoarse cry was tinged with panic. 'There's some guy been knifed down Laguna Street.'

Johnny Concho!

Straight away, some sixth sense told Del it was his partner. He rushed into the street and grabbed hold of the alarmed man.

'Is he dead?' The query emerged as a raspy croak.

'Sure l-looks that w-way,' stammered the frightened

man. 'He sure ain't goin' no place.' Then he hurried off in the direction of the marshal's office.

Del felt sick. One minute he was ready to celebrate his good fortune, the next plunged into the depths of despair. He stood in the middle of the dark street, unable to move. The killing had to be a robbery. Some rats must have learned about the dough and lured Johnny down that alley.

His head hung low on his chest. Blue eyes misted over with tears. Not for the money: he ought not to have entrusted the kid with so much responsibility. It was his doing. Guilt washed over the hardened Texan. Johnny Concho was dead because of him.

'You know somethin' about this killin', mister?'

The gruff demand came from a grizzled man whose lined face hinted at hard times past. Clu Taggart might have given the impression that he was over the hill, but the upright stance and stoical regard told Del this was a guy not to be messed with.

Before he had a chance to reply, two men emerged from the alley carrying the body of Johnny Concho on a stretcher. Del hustled across. Signalling the duo to stop, he peered down at the wan face of his young partner. A single teardrop etched a trail down his cheek.

Laying a trembling hand on the kid's thatch of straw hair, he whispered, 'Don't you worry, son, I'll get the skunks what done this if'n it's the last thing I do.' A brief frown crossed the ashen countenance. 'You boys find a hat down there?' he enquired of the two corpsemen.

Both men shook their heads. 'There weren't nothing only this, mister.'

One of the men produced the wicked-looking knife that he had removed from the kid's back. Streaks of dried blood stained the glinting blade.

Johnny's blood.

Del sucked in a deep lungful of air to steady his nerves. So one of the bastards had taken the kid's pride and joy. His eyes narrowed to thin slits. The tight line of his pursed lips spoke of vengeance to be meted out. And that meant finding the current owner of the distinctive black hat with its ring of silver conchos. Only then would he have found the killer.

'You obviously know this guy,' said the marshal butting in on Del's vindictive thoughts. 'I need you to fill me in if'n I'm gonna have a chance of catching the killer.'

Del nodded, his head sank dejectedly on his chest as the pair moved down the street in the wake of the corpsemen. The grisly cortège was watched by numerous muttering onlookers. Yuma was no stranger to such brutal occurrences, despite the close proximity of the infamous prison. But each brutal slaying only served to remind those still around of their precarious hold on life in this wild and barbaric land.

Over a mug of strong coffee laced with a generous measure of whiskey, Del relayed the events leading up to their arrival in Yuma. Halfway through his narration, the door of the office opened and a bustling rotund jasper clad in a white apron entered.

'Howdy, Fred,' said the marshal. 'You seem in an all-fired hurry.'

'I just seen the body of that kid, Marshal,' the sweating man replied hurriedly. 'He was in the Border Post early on this evening. Had a few drinks and was flashing a wad of dough around. Somebody must have seen it and reckoned on some easy pickings.'

'Did you see anybody follow him outside when he left?' asked Taggart sipping his coffee.

The barman shook his head. 'Too busy serving drinks, Marshal. Could have been anyone. Sorry.'

Taggart nodded. 'Anyway, thanks for telling me.'

'Just figured you ought to know.'

After the bartender had left, Taggart hoisted himself to his feet. It was the signal that the interview was over.

'I'll do my darnedest to apprehend who's responsible, Mr Gannon,' he muttered, in a less than optimistic tone. 'But my figuring is that he'll have made tracks and left town. Like as not heading for the border. Ain't no chance of catching him once he's in Mexico.' He shrugged his shoulders. 'All I can do is ride out in the morning and see if I can pick up his trail.'

Del expected as much. Taggart meant well. But guys like him were more used to breaking up fights and rolling drunks than hunting down ellusive killers. No mention had been made of the lost hat. Del Gannon intended making it his life's work to seek out the skunk who was now wearing it. Johnny's killer would pay the ultimate price for his foul deed.

More immediate, however, was the fact that he was broke. With the money stolen, he would not be able to fulfil his dream of growing oranges in California. A hand strayed to his pockets.

Empty. Not even enough for a shot to drown his sorrows.

Idly, Del wandered down the street. After collecting his horse, he sauntered morosely to the edge of town where he'd spotted a livery stable. Perhaps the ostler would allow him to bed down in a vacant stall with his horse. This was the poorer part of the town. And it sure smelt like it too. Again Del cursed his ill-fortune.

There was nobody in the barn so he took advantage of the chance for a free night's lodging.

It was a far cry from his original intention of occupying a feather bed in the swankiest hotel in Yuma that night. But at least he still had some grub to keep him going, even if it was only beef jerky.

Chewing on a stick of the basic fare, he pondered over his altered circumstances. One minute with the world at his feet, the next reduced to sleeping rough with a bleak future in prospect. And his partner dead.

A lesser man might have drowned in self-pity. Del Gannon was made from sterner stuff. An icy glint probed the darkness of the stable. All that sustained the ex-bronc buster now was finding the varmint who had destroyed his future and killed young Johnny.

With that stubborn notion sustaining him, the Texan bedded down in the straw. But sleep eluded the anxious man. Nightmares haunted his throbbing brain. Not until the early hours did he finally manage to drop off.

A crowing rooster jerked him awake as the false dawn edged a path over the eastern rim of the nearby Growler Mountains. A pale-orange glow slowly swelled as the new day advanced across the land. Time to depart before the ostler appeared.

Del quickly saddled up and was on his way before anyone in the town was abroad. Only a lone dog crossed his trail. The mangy cur emitted a suspicious growl. Del snarled back. A seething anger gripped his heart. He had no idea which way the killer could have gone.

All he could do now was head further west and hope to pick up his trail in the next town.

FOUR

LONE WOLF

It took Del five days to reach Superstition.

By then his small supply of food was almost exhausted. Sourdough biscuits and beef jerky might just about keep body and soul together, but they sure didn't excite the taste buds. Mouth-watering visions of prime beef steaks smothered in fried potatoes haunted his dreams.

Nor were these culinary fantasies confined to the night. By the time he reached the border town on the edge of the desert, Del was suffering from mirages in which succulent food played a key role. In order to assuage these tormenting reveries, he knew that something would have to be hocked to raise much-needed dough.

And the only thing of any value he now possessed was the 1866 Henry rifle. No longer a new weapon, it was reliable and the brass frame with silver plating gave it added distinction. He hauled the rifle out of its leather scabbard. Caressing the pitted rosewood stock, he untied his bandanna and vigorously polished the smooth wood and etched metal surfaces of the gun.

Del was loath to sell the rifle, not just on account of its value; a lever-action repeater gave much better protection. The 1863 Army Remington revolver converted to cartridge use was effective at close range. But it would not raise the cash essential for the continued search for Johnny Concho's killer.

The need to secure funds was brought home with a bang as he passed the open door of a diner. Irresistible smells of juicy food drifted on the still air. An overwhelming seduction to a hungry man. Opposite the diner was a second-hand goods store. Most towns possessed one. They served a useful purpose for travellers down on their luck.

Del wasted no time. Leaping off his jaded mount, he hustled inside the dimly lit emporium. It was filled will all manner of goods that folks had left for a fraction of their value.

The jingling doorbell saw a sour-faced clerk looking up from the ledger he was completing. A sniff of disdain greeted the dust-caked visitor. There was no disguising the contempt in which he was held. Just another saddle tramp wanting some extra drinking money.

Exuding a deliberate snort of impatience, the clerk laid down his pen and eyed the newcomer without speaking.

Del held his rising temper in check with some effort. The impulse to grab the toad's scrawny neck and twist until his eyes popped was resisted. He was here to do business. And that required a measure of detached handling. Casually he placed the rifle on the counter.

Raised eyebrows declared the question more than words.

With a slow deliberation, the clerk picked up the gun and began to examine it. Negative shakes of the head and clicks of the tongue followed – expected stocks in trade from such dealers. He worked the action and sighted down the barrel. Nothing wrong there. To conclude, he took out a lens and peered closely at the silver etching. This at least caused a brief show of approval. Then the austere frown quickly returned.

Slowly he placed the gun back on the counter. A deliberate stroking of the long pointed chin followed.

'Can't give you more'n ten bucks,' he announced brusquely.

A tinge of red suffused Del's burning cheeks. 'The carving alone is worth twice that,' he snapped, before quickly moderating his tone. 'And it shoots real good. That gun was given to me by Kit Carson himself after we squashed the Cheyenne at Beecher Island in Colorado. I was one of the scouts.'

Receiving the gun after a handful of volunteer army scouts had beaten off 600 blood-thirsty Indians had been a proud moment for the Texan. And he was damned if'n he was going to surrender his prized firearm for such a paltry sum.

'That ain't no concern of mine,' huffed the trader, peering imperiously over his spectacles. 'I have to consider what this gun will sell for.'

Although he had to admit that the revelation concerning the weapon's origins would make for a profitable selling point. And the etching was certainly pure silver. However, he concealed these notions behind the blank stare. This gun would not be gathering dust on his shelves for long.

The two men eyed each other, neither wanting to give an inch.

Del was first to make a move. Hawking out a grunt of irritation, he picked up the rifle and turned to leave.

The toad was taken aback by the sudden move. His jaw dropped. He wanted that gun: it would sell for at least thirty bucks.

'Tell you what I'll do,' he said, in a far more conciliatory manner. 'And I'm going out on a limb here.' The guy paused for effect as if reconsidering his rash decision. 'Go on then. I'm feeling mighty generous today. Twenty bucks. Take it or leave it.' He slapped his hands on the counter.

Del smiled as he handed the gun to the trader.

Ten minutes later, he was seated in the diner ordering the largest meal on the menu. A pot of prime grade coffee helped neutralize the rancid taste of stale biscuits and dried beef clinging to the inside of his throat before the meal arrived. Savouring every mouthful, Del took his time, finishing with a large slice of apple pie.

Revitalized, he needed to buy a pack mule and some supplies to continue his pursuit of the killer. But Del's first call was to the local law office.

A young guy was busy pinning up some notices. Jeff Hogan was a deputy sheriff. His boss was enjoying a day off.

'Howdy, mister.' Hogan greeted the visitor with an easy smile. 'Some'n I can do for you?'

'Just wondering if'n a fella wearing a black hat has passed through here in the last few days,' Del quizzed the lawman.

'Plenty of dudes come through Superstition,' Hogan replied, shrugging his shoulders. 'How am I supposed to remember one guy with a black hat?' He turned back to continue with his task.

'This hat was different,' persisted Del. 'It had a ring of silver conchos. Can't be many like that.'

Hogan paused to reconsider. 'You could be right at that,' he murmured thoughtfully scratching his chin. 'Three fellas came through two days back. One of them could be the guy you're after. A friend of your'n?'

Del's rugged features tightened. Three killers! The steely glint in his eyes did not pass unnoticed.

'Guess they ain't,' was Hogan's cautious response. 'You need the law to help find them?'

Del shook his head. Dealing with the three killers was something he intended handling alone. 'All I need is for you to tell me which direction they took out of town.'

'There's only one way out of Superstition,' replied Hogan, 'and that's north-west across the Algodones.' The young lawman studied his older visitor closely. 'A man should think twice before crossing that arid wilderness. Only a fool or a man on the run would try it.'

Del ignored the comment.

'Much obliged, Deputy,' he said heading for the door. 'That's all I needed to know.'

A rolling expanse of shifting dunes, the Algodones had claimed the lives of many who had attempted to cross the ocean of sand. The only watering hole was six days' ride to the north-west. Harper's Well was no more than a tiny spring on the edge of the Salton Sink.

Del wiped the sweat from his brow. Hopefully he would have caught up with the killers before then.

The approach to the dunes lay along a winding arroyo. Parched and dry, it had clearly not held any water for some time. Del tugged on the rope attached to his pack mule. The animal had stopped to chew on a clump of dessicated bindweed. Its load had cost him most of the dough obtained by selling his Henry rifle.

'Come on, yuh lazy critter,' muttered Del. 'Ain't no use hanging back. The sooner we cross them dunes, the better for us both.' Another tug jerked the animal back into motion.

That was when a high-pitched yahoo assailed his

ears. Muted and indistinct, it appeared to be coming from the far side of a cluster of rocks on the right side of the arroyo. He paused. The mule saw the stoppage as an opportunity to resume its meal.

Del pricked up his ears. Perhaps it had been the wind playing tricks.

'Aaaaagh!'

There it was again. Del tensed. That howl was definately of human origin. And with a tremulous inflection indicating the owner was in serious trouble, a conclusion supported by a raucous laugh.

Somebody was being attacked.

Tying the mule's lead rope to a clump of mesquite, Del spurred his mount up the side of the arroyo and around the edge of the rocks where he drew rein.

Down below in a shallow depression beyond were three white men. They were taunting an Indian youth.

But this was no affable funning. The boy was scared stiff. He was no more than fourteen. A dead animal close by indicated that he must have been out hunting when these bully boys attacked him.

They had each thrown a rope over him and were now pulling and tugging, dragging their victim along the rough ground. A series of ribald guffaws accompanied the rough-house treatment.

What stayed Del's immediate intervention was not the unfavourable odds: one of the assailants was wearing a black hat with silver conchos. Del rubbed his eyes and squinted out the heat-haze to confirm his suspicion.

No doubt about it: that was Johnny's hat!

So these varmints had to be his killers.

For a brief moment the realization of having stumbled across them so soon in his vengeful quest acted as a stunning jolt. But Del quickly shook off the numbing trauma. What to do about it? That was the question now assailing his thoughts. Silently, the watcher considered how best to tackle the cowardly bushwhackers.

Mouthing a muffled curse at having sold his rifle, Del drew his pistol and checked the load. He would need to get closer for it to be effective.

One of the men had drawn his own revolver. The bullies had clearly tired of their sadistic game and were intent on finishing in the usual way of chicken-livered yellow bellies. Blooded and half dead already, the boy was about to be despatched to the happy hunting grounds before his time.

Immediate action was needed if he was to be saved.

Girding himself up, Del sucked in a lungful of air. Pistol palmed and ready, he dug in his spurs. The chestnut leapt forward. It ate up the ground at a leg-stretching gallop.

The first shot punched Mad Dog Regan out of the saddle. He was dead before he hit the ground. Two more from Del's smokepole missed, by which time, Reaper had swung his own gun to address this sudden threat. One of his bullets scored a furrow acoss the shoulder of Del's horse. The animal reared up, throwing its rider to the ground.

Del was on his feet in an instant. Both men faced

each other in the open.

Frantically cocking and firing, Reaper stayed on his horse. The deafening exchange did nothing to calm the terrified creature. It bucked and whinnied, throwing off its rider's aim. That gave Del the chance to make his own shots count. But he only had one bullet left.

He took careful aim.

The final slug took the outlaw in the shoulder. It was not a fatal hit, Reaper was only wounded. But the killer was unable to maintain his balance in the saddle. He slid sideways tumbling on to the hot sand.

The frightened horse reared up. Reaper didn't stand a chance. He was trampled to death beneath the stomping hoofs of his panic-stricken cayuse.

Meanwhile, Cabel Sharkey had taken the opportunity to quit the battlefield. The outlaw was no hero. With two men down, he knew that he could be next in the sights of the mysterious gunman. And in any case, he was carrying the stolen money bag.

A rising plume of dust told Del the direction his enemy was taking. But there was no chance for him to continue with the pursuit. His horse was wounded. And the Indian boy needed treatment.

After checking the saddle packs of the two dead outlaws, he was able to confirm that the fleeing brigand was in possession of his stolen money. Lady Luck was still giving him the cold shoulder. He shook an impotent fist at the disappearing dust cloud.

A group of prairie dogs stood by in silent observation of this strange intruder before disappearing back into their burrow.

Del then turned his attention to the boy.

He lay in a crumpled heap on the far side of the depression. He was unconscious. Del hurried across praying he hadn't cashed in his chips. Thankfully, none of his injuries were life threatening. He was badly bruised and covered in minor lacerations, but the blood made him look far worse than was the case.

Gently the Texan hoisted the boy into his arms and carried him over to where the chestnut was standing. The animal's glazed eyes and nodding head attested to it being in considerable pain.

'The kid first, Red.' Del stroked the injured animal's muzzle. 'You'll just have to stand in line.'

The chestnut gave a neighing reply. He could wait.

Del unhooked the water bottle and dribbled some of the life-giving fluid between the boy's cracked lips.

Flickering eyelids opened as the youth slowly regained consciousness. Fear registered at the sight of another white man. His trembling body drew away.

'No need to be frightened, kid,' the rescuer assured him. 'I ain't gonna harm you.' The mollifying tone appeared to calm the boy. Although it was a further ten minutes before he was ready to answer any questions put to him by his rescuer.

Del tried his own spoken language.

But it received nought but a blank regard. So he next resorted to the form of communication developed by the northern plains tribes hoping it had drifted this far south.

Sign language had spread rapidly among the

various tribes and had proved to be highly successful for passing on all manner of messages. Del had learned it from an old Sioux chief. Iron Hand told him that while the Great Spirit gave the white man power to read and write, he gave Indians the power to talk with hands and arms. It soon evolved into the most expressive and versatile of silent communcation ever known.

The boy was quick to respond.

His name was Lone Wolf and he hailed from the Yuma tribe. He had indeed been on a solo hunting expedition when the three bushwhackers had surprised him while skinning a mule deer brought down with a well-placed arrow. The tribal village lay three days' ride to the north.

The men had berated him and become ever more incensed when he refused to respond to their blunt interrogation. With only a bow and arrow for protection against three heavily armed men, he stood no chance. Agitated hand movements emphasized the fear engendered by the attack. Doleful eyes told his white rescuer how grateful he was for the intervention.

Del responded by falling back into his own tongue.

'Ain't never been able to close my eyes to bulldozing,' he said dribbling more water into the kid's mouth. The boy stared back expressionless. 'Main thing now is to fix up your wounds and head back to your village pronto.'

Moving across to the pack mule, he dug out a

bottle of horse liniment and proceeded to clean up the myriad of cuts and abrasions covering the kid's body. 'This stuff works wonders on a cayuse. Ain't no reason it can't do the same for human injuries.'

A half-hour later, the boy was clinging to the back of his saviour on the chestnut. His own mount had stampeded and would no doubt find its way back to the village in due course.

Riding double with an injured passenger, progress was slow. In consequence, it was four days before the small Yuma village came in sight.

FIVE

THE BLACK STONES

Half-a-dozen braves armed with lances and bows escorted the two riders into the Indian encampment. Initially they had intended staking out the white man on witnessing the bloodstained figure of the youngster. Only the boy's swift intervention in his own tongue prevented a miscarriage of justice.

One of the braves had then ridden ahead to inform the chief of their imminent arrival.

Painted Tail stood at the entrance to his wikiup. Upright and motionless like a statue carved from rock, the Yuma indian chief surveyed the approaching party. His leathery features were scoured and ribbed by the dry desert wind. And held across his chest was an ancient Northwest musket. Dating back to the early part of the century, its barrel was pitted with rust. Whether it would fire, Del had serious doubts.

The ageing warrior had been worried that his son had been attacked by a mountain lion or fallen down a ravine. This hunting trip had been the boy's initiation into survival in the wild, a rite of passage which all young men had to experience in order to prove their manhood.

He greeted Lone Wolf with reserved warmth as was expected from a tribal chieftain. The boy explained in his own tongue what had occurred and how the white-eyes had come to his aid. The boy beckoned his saviour to come forward. Greetings were exchanged.

A medicine man was then summoned and Lone Wolf was led away to have his wounds tended as prescribed by Yuma tradition. Del knew that many of these age-old remedies had much to recommend them.

The chief expressed his gratitude in the white man's tongue. Painted Tail was one of only a handful in the tribe thus able to communicate. As a scout for the army operating out of Bender's Fort, picking up the strange vernacular had been essential to maintain the prestigious job.

'I am much grateful to you, Gannon, for helping my son,' he intoned with a solemn dignity, bowing low as he spoke. The rest of those present did the same. Del responded in a like manner. 'The bodies of those killed can feed the scavengers of the desert.' He spat the words into the dust. A murmur of accord greeted the brusque comment.

Painted Tail signalled for the elders to sit round the fire. Their honoured guest held pride of place beside the tribal leader.

A wave of the old chief's hand instantly produced a friendship pipe. It was a long hardwood tube and decorated with beading and eagle feathers. A lighted taper was applied to the bowl whereupon Painted Tail proceeded to draw deeply until the mixture of tobacco and various aromatic herbs was burning properly to his satisfaction.

Then he passed it to his guest.

Del took a few puffs of the power-packed concoction ensuring that he did not cough. Such a misdemeanour would have lowered his status in the eyes of the gathering. Exhaling the smoke was intended as a breath of prayer to the gods for returning Lone Wolf safely to the tribe.

'You stay here tonight, eat and drink to celebrate son's return.'

It was an order rather than a request. Del had no option but to accept. A stoical regard effectively concealed his impatience.

He would have much preferred to get on his way in pursuit of the surviving killer. Such a thirsting for revenge would have to be temporarily curtailed, the hope being that it would be for no more than a day or two. Although he had known Indian celebrations to go on for a week.

With each hour that passed, Cabel Sharkey was getting further away, his trail fading.

Thankfully the feast only lasted for two days.

On the third day, Del was anxious to leave. But he could not hurry things. Indians operated at a much more sedate pace than whites. Del mused that his own people could learn much from such a way of life. Nontheless, impatience gnawed at his vitals.

At long last, the final goodbyes were expressed.

As he made to mount his horse, the pack mule restocked with all manner of delicacies, Painted Tail handed him a small hemp bag.

'These for you, Gannon,' the deep voice rumbled. 'Will bring luck and successful end to your hunt for last bad guy.'

Del unfastened the bag and tipped some of the contents into his hand. He suppressed a puzzled frown.

A number of shiny black stones lay in the palm of his hand. They felt quite heavy for their size and looked like pieces of coal. He had no idea what they were but smiled his thanks at the chief.

'Gannon is very grateful for generosity of Painted Tail,' he replied with an equal measure of sobriety. 'These stones will for sure help me to chase down the varmint and gain revenge for the killing of my friend and the evil treatment of your son.'

He tipped the unusual stones back into the bag and placed them in his saddle-bag. And there they were to remain for some considerable time. Ignored and forgotten.

An hour after leaving the Yuma encampment, Del

had reached the notorious expanse of sand known as the Algodones Dunes. He had no fear of crossing the treacherous ocean of sand. Painted Tail had given him three full goatskins of fresh water. Everything went fine until his second day out when the animals became bogged down. The rapacious sand was as menacing as any snowbank that he had experienced in the Rockies.

A detour was necessary to reach firmer ground beyond. The grim toil exhausted both man and beasts forcing a day's halt to recover.

That was when a brutal wind sprang up.

One minute the air was still and clear. The next, a cloud of dust blotted out the blazing sun forcing Del to hunker down behind the crouched bodies of his animals. The sand storm lasted for two days after which it passed on swiftly disappearing like a wraith in the night.

The journey continued. But water supplies were running low. There was only half a skin left. And no sign of the dunes coming to an end. Each hill of sand that was crested revealed yet another on the far side. An endless wasteland with the delusive mirages forever taunting the jaded rider, laughing at his puny efforts.

He knew that the lakes of shimmering water ahead were merely tantalizing figments of his imagination. But still he hoped, urging the tired chestnut onward, knowing deep down that the lake could never be reached.

Finally after eight days, he stumbled out of the

desert, his goatskins empty. The Salton Sink was a flat salty plain, glaringly white. But a small rocky outcrop on the edge concealed the spring of water which Painted Tail had described to him.

Had the Yuma chieftain not mentioned it, he would have surely passed it by unnoticed. Thankfully, it was no illusion.

Harper's Well had earned its name as it was the only source of water this side of the salt flats. It was named after Drip Dry Harper who had first discovered it. The crazy jigger had a habit of washing in creeks fully clothed then letting the sun dry him out.

Del uttered a silent prayer of thanks to the guy, and to his Maker for guiding him to the tiny oasis.

And where there is water, other forms of life are able to flourish. Delicate red poppy blooms intermingled with the hardier grey green creosote bushes, while the fluffy heads of teddy bear chollas added a sense of well-being to the tranquil scene.

Tumbling off his horse, Del threw himself into the modest rock pool. Old Drip Dry would have loved that. The cooling water quickly revived his flagging spirits. The animals did not need any second bidding to join him. Thick leathery tongues avidly lapped up the life-giving elixir.

Sitting on the edge of the spring beside a fire that night, he finished the last of the tasty cakes made from mescal and wild cherries that had been presented to him by Painted Tail's wife. A final cigar over a cup of coffee, then he settled down for the night.

Staring up at the broad canopy of stars overhead,

Del debated with himself whether the killer of Johnny Concho had managed to make it across the Algodones. He had no idea which of the three no-goods had knifed his young buddy. And he didn't care. They had all been party to the heinous crime. Two had paid the full price. The third would follow.

With that final thought lodged in his mind, the avenging crusader fell into a dreamless sleep.

Up at first light, Del headed due west along the southern edge of the Salton Sink. Around midday he found the first clue telling him that he was on the right trail.

A dead mule. The scraggy remains, half eaten by coyotes, still had the owner's supply pack attached. Surely it must have belonged to his quarry. Del's face cracked in a grim smile of satisfaction. The guy must have missed the vital spring.

How long would it be afore he stumbled across the killer's remains?

Narrowed eyes scanned the horizon. No sign of any human presence. Just an endless wilderness of rock and sand.

The avenger continued onward. Three days later the terrain slowly began to change. From the dull ochre and browns of the desert, a welcome hint of greenery made its influence felt. Palo verde trees and cottonwoods indicated that life was returning to the sterile land. And then he noticed a herd of goats. Soon after he entered a tract of grassland, parched and brown, but sufficient to feed the tough creatures.

Another day passed before Del came across the first human being he had encountered for two weeks. A goatherd with his small flock stood in the doorway of an old shack. He was pointing a Hawken long rifle at the newcomer. Del raised both his arms to show he meant no harm.

'If you come in peace, then step down, stranger,' said the old buzzard laying aside the gun. 'A fella can't be too careful these days.' He held out a hand in greeting. 'Jock Campbell's the name.'

'Del Gannon,' replied his visitor shaking the proffered hand. His mouth twisted in puzzlement while staring at the strange headgear perched on the man's mop of grey hair. 'Cain't seem to place that accent. You sure ain't from around these parts. Kentucky by any chance?'

Campbell emitted a croaky guffaw revealing a mouth of broken teeth. 'Scotland!!' exclaimed the goatherd. 'And this here hat you find so amusing is a tam-o'-shanter made in the pattern of the Campbell tartan.'

Del nodded.

'Anyways,' continued Campbell, lighting up an old briar pipe. 'I don't see more'n a handful of jiggers passing through here in a year. More fellas are draped over their saddles than are sat on 'em. Then two come along in the same number of weeks.'

Del's ears pricked up.

Campbell noticed his visitor's sudden interest.

'This other jigger a friend of your'n?' The query was spat out.

'Friend ain't the word I'd use for that critter,' Del snorted, an icy gleam prodding the man. 'He killed my partner. You don't seem too taken with the rat yourself.'

'That's cos he shot my dog.' Campbell's head drooped. 'Old Butch was only after lickin' his hand and the bastard guns the poor mutt down.'

The old guy shrugged off his dour thoughts. 'You look about all in, Del,' he observed, inviting the weary traveller into his shack for a simple home-cooked meal of tortillas and goat's meat.

'How far is the main town?' asked the newcomer accepting a tin mug of home-made whiskey while mouthing a forkful of pumpkin pie.

'Borrego ain't no more'n three days' ride to the north-west,' drawled the old-timer refilling Del's mug. 'There's a rodeo takin' place on the edge of town for the next few days, so the place is buzzin' at the moment.' The goatherd gave a derisive sniff. 'Not for me. I prefer the company of my goats to a passel of high and mighty bronc riders struttin' around.'

Del concealed a smile. But he was anxious to get on his way and reach civilization, then he could hopefully catch up with his prey.

He thanked the old man for his hospitality. Just as he was leaving, a thought occurred to him. He reined up and turned round.

'What did this other fella look like?' he asked.

Campbell considered a moment stroking his whiskery chin. 'Big guy hiding behind a thick black beard. Wore a couple of pistols in crossdraw holsters.

A real mean-eyed cuss if ever I saw one. Didn't stop but to refill his canteen. And shoot my dog.' Another growling curse rumbled in the whiskey-soured throat before he resumed. 'Seemed awful keen to reach Borrego. Said he had work lined up there.'

Del's face darkened.

'*Adios*, old-timer.' He tipped his hat to the friendly Scot. 'Much obliged for the grub.'

Then, without another word, he swung round and spurred off in the direction of Borrego. A shouted comment from Jock Campbell saw him hauling rein.

'You find that no-good piece of crap.' The anger was translated into the old goatherd's vitriolic retort. 'And make sure he gets an extra bullet from Butch and me.'

'I'll add it to my list of grievances,' Del replied, with a wave of acknowledgement.

SIX

ONE IN A THOUSAND

Del could hear the noise generated by the rodeo long before the town of Borrego came in sight. Whoops and yahoos mingled with the raucous bawling of hogtied steers and the neighing of wild broncs. He spurred the chestnut to a canter eager to feast his peepers on the recently introduced spectacle.

Rodeos had always attracted the bronc-peeler since he had attended the first one at Cheyenne, up in Wyoming territory back in '72. The rodeo, from the Spanish meaning round-up, began in Mexico. They were more like fiestas that combined the skills of the *vaquero* with much dancing and eating. Many of them often went on for a whole week.

California was always recognized as the home of

roping skills and it was here that they flourished.

Del was especially interested in the contest where riders had to stay seated on a bucking mustang for a stated length of time. He had become one of the top riders before a bad fall had injured a leg.

The entire eastern side of the town had been commandeered by the rodeo. Corrals and holding pens had been set up to accommodate all the animals. To one side a tent city housed competitors who had come from far and wide to take part in the prestigious event.

Other establishments advertised all manner of gear and equipment for sale relating to the skills being performed. Saddlers, feed stores and ropemakers stood beside a blacksmith specializing in custom-made branding irons. And to wash away the dust of the arena, the inevitable host of drinking tents.

Del nudged his horse down the main thoroughfare and tied off at a hitching rail at the end.

He strolled back up the temporary highway, eyes flitting back and forth between the the array of entertainments and displays on show.

Passing one stall, a cheery voice caught his attention.

'Excuse me, sir,' warbled a lilting southern dialect. 'You look like a fellow who would appreciate this fine example of weaponry I am intending to give away in the near future.'

Del paused in mid-stride. He slanted a wary glance at the speaker.

Foxy Jim Tucker was a typical fairground barker. Flashily clad in check pants and a red silk vest, a waxed moustache glued beneath the beaky snout gave the lean face a rat-like mien. The bizarre sight was topped off by a beaverskin top hat perched on the weasel's thatch of greasy black hair.

But what grabbed Del's attention was what he was holding. Tucker noted the drifter's interest.

'You see here one of the most sought after rifles produced by the firearms company of Oliver Winchester.' He pushed the gun towards the new-comer. 'Feel it, sir. Try the action. This is a special gun: one of a thousand that Mr Winchester has judged to be far more accurate and finely balanced than any other rifle ever produced.' The barker exuded an exaggerated sigh. 'Truly a noble work of art, I'm sure you will agree.'

'Sure is one smart-looking weapon,' agreed Del admiring the intricate silver carving as he caressed the polished mahogany stock. It made his own Henry pale into insignificance. Then he remembered that he no longer owned a long gun. He eyed the barker suspiciously. 'What would I have to do to obtain this rifle?'

'Many have admired and praised the gun, just like yourself. A contest has been in progress all week to find a worthy owner. This afternoon will be your last chance to enter.'

Del waited for the unctous varmint to continue.

'All it will cost you is a five-dollar entrance fee.' Tucker held out a hand expecting to receive the stated amount. 'A paltry sum for a gun that would fetch over one hundred dollars on the open market.'

Del felt in his pockets, knowing that the fee might just as well have been fifty bucks. He was stony broke. All that emerged in his hand was the bag containing the black stones. He almost threw them away. They hadn't brought him any luck so far. Only the kindness of the Yuma Indians prevented their being ditched.

'I'll owe you the money if'n you'll let me enter,' he said hopefully.

Tucker laughed. It was a scornful hoot of derision.

'And what makes you think that you will be the winner?' he mocked, stepping back and placing the rifle back into its tooled leather scabbard. 'Many others are taking part. And there can only be one winner.' He gave a scornful click of the tongue. 'No credit here, buster. If'n you ain't got the fee, you can't enter the contest. Now beat it before I call the rodeo boss and have you thrown off the site.'

Without waiting for a response, the barker then resumed his sales pitch to attract other interested passers-by. Del moved away, seething with anger and itching to relieve his pent-up frustration.

But how?

Ten minutes later he found himself outside a large ring where the bronc riding was taking place. Climbing up the wooden palisade, he perched himself on the top rail. His lofty position was close to where the riders emerged from the constricted pen. Inside wild mustangs were tethered in readiness for their potential riders.

One goggle-eyed young cowpoke was in the saddle. A look of pure terror was etched across the ashen features.

A signal from the steward and the gate was flung open. Instantly, horse and rider erupted into the arena. Wildly bucking for all it was worth, the irate untamed mustang desperately threw itself all over the ring trying to unseat its unwelcome passenger.

Urged on by the rowdy excitement of the crowd, the 'puncher desperately hung on. The best riders always tried to put on a show for the audience by waving their hats with a free hand. Most, however, were forced to cling on for dear life, just like this fella. Barely lasting more than a few seconds, he was unceremoniously dumped on to the hard ground.

At this point stewards dressed in clown costumes dashed into the arena to distract the animal while the stunned ex-rider was led away. Most of the contestants suffered nothing but a few bruises and a dented ego. But broken bones were not uncommon, so a sawbones always had to be in close attendance.

Bronc riding was a dangerous event in which only the toughest survived.

Del watched while five more riders tried to stay in the saddle. Only one managed to succeed.

'How much to enter?' he asked a passing steward.

'Three bucks,' the man called back, as he hurried off to rescue yet another poor sap who was chewing dust.

Even that was too much for Del.

Morosely he surveyed the next bronc being levered into the holding cage. It was wilder than any of the others. Hoofs thrashed and beat at the wooden poles threatening to bust out of the cage. The animal was a beautiful black stallion that everyone had thus far refused to mount. Fear of being trampled to death far outwayed the chance of winning forty bucks.

One of the stewards was heard to remark, 'Anybody rides this old boy for just five seconds, let alone the customary twelve, deserves to win.'

'Can't disagree with you there, Frank,' another concurred sadly shaking his head. 'But there ain't nobody willing nor able to take him on.'

Del quickly stepped down and approached the two officials.

'I'll ride him!'

The blunt remark found the pair of stewards sceptically appraising the dust-stained saddle tramp. The guy sure didn't look like a bronc rider. Scuffed boots, torn Levis, and ten days' stubble did not evince any confidence in his avowed claim.

'And not only that, I'll stay on his back for the full twelve seconds.' Del's presumptuous air of superiority meant nothing to the rodeo stewards. Dubious scowls prompted the newcomer to suggest a compromise. 'Give me a chance,' he pleaded, desperation written across the tanned visage. 'I ain't got the entry fee but I'll split the prize money with you when I win.' He eyed the two men, hopefully adding, 'What have you got to lose?'

The optimistic appeal urged the two men to agree to the unusual suggestion.

Frank Binns glanced at his partner. 'What d'yuh reckon, Tubb? Should we give him a try?'

Tubb Hoskins shrugged. 'Ten bucks each if'n he wins. We can't lose.'

'He's all your'n, mister,' said Binns. 'I just hope yuh know what you're takin' on with Black Magic.'

Before he'd finished speaking, Del had scrambled up on to the top rail of the cage. Balancing above the snorting mound of black sinew and muscle, he prepared to launch himself on to the choleric animal's back. Nerves strung tight, he waited for just the right moment.

Then he jumped.

'Let him go, boys!' he yelled.

Franks Binns pulled back the bolt and the gate swung open. Black Magic immediately sensed freedom. The stallion bounded into the arena. Hoofs madly thrashing, every muscle straining to the limit, the angry beast bucked and twisted, desperately trying to unseat its uninvited load.

But the rider stubbornly refused to leave. Seconds ticked by – five, six, seven. . . .

The stallion became increasingly more aggressive. Its nostrels flared. The strong back arched as it leapt high into the air descending to earth with a mighty crash that was intended to remove any rider.

But Del Gannon remained firmly in control.

Ten, eleven, twelve.

Somewhere in the outside world beyond his

intense concentration, a bell rang signalling the end of the contest. But Del kept going. He had no intention of releasing his hold over the fiery animal until it realized who was in charge here.

Slowly, Black Magic simmered down. A full minute passed before he was being ridden around the arena to a fanfare of cheering and adulation. Nobody had ever witnessed anything like it.

Sliding out of the saddle, he handed the reins to a bemused Tubb Hoskins.

'Never thought I'd see Magic get tamed like that,' drawled his stunned associate. 'Reckon you earned the full prize for that display of bustin', fella. What d'yuh say, Tubb?'

Hoskins could only nod his agreement. The bemused expression signified that nothing short of a miracle had just occurred.

'Never thought I'd see the day. . . .' Binns reiterated scratching his head.

'And taming him like that . . . well. . . .' Hoskins was also lost for words.

'You must have done this before, mister,' Binns said sticking his hand into the cash bag. He counted out the wad of notes and handed them across to an elated Del Gannon.

'I worked for Jake Bundy over in the Eagletails breaking wild mustangs for the army.'

The two rodeo men looked at one another. Now they understood.

'That explains a lot,' nodded Hoskins.

'We used to run with Jake ourselves before quitting

to start up these rodeo events,' Binns added. 'He sure is one helluva bronc peeler.'

'Sure taught me all I know,' agreed Del once again. Hand in pocket, he once again felt the strange presence of the black stones. Maybe his luck was turning after all.

Then he ambled away anxious to register for the shooting contest.

The barker's beady eye dubiously appraised the approaching drifter. 'Got the entry fee yet?' he snorted.

Del held the simpering toad's imperious regard before slamming a five-dollar bill down on the stall counter.

'So let's get to it,' Del grunted pushing past the barker into the fenced off compound.

Five other shooters were ranged behind a line. Each had been supplied with a regular .44.40 Winchester carbine. Later termed 'The Gun that Won the West', it bore no resemblance to the prize on offer.

The aim of the contest was to knock all five tin cans off a pole at a distance of fifty yards. A single miss and the competitor was immediately eliminated. Those that succeeded, passed through to the next round.

Of the five contestants, only one managed the task.

Then Del accepted the gun from a steward and checked it for sight and balance before stepping up to the firing line. Taking careful aim, he went along the line in a slow sweep effectively despatching the targets into the air. Smoke twisted from the barrel as he handed the gun back to the attendant. Then he waited over to one side for the next round of shooting.

Ten minutes later, the first five men were called forward.

An attendant addressed them giving precise instructions.

'This time, boys, the targets are at seventy-five yards and you have to hit eight out of ten.' He waited for the contestants to nod their understanding.

'Only two men can go through on this round. So it's speed as well as accuracy that's being tested here. Start firing when I lower the flag to the ground.' A watchful eye peered along the line of shooters. 'Go before my signal and you'll be disqualified.'

The shooters took up their stance, rifles firmly clamped to shoulders. The flag was raised above the attendant's head.

'Ready!'

As soon as it touched the ground, an ear-shattering roar erupted from the line of blasting rifles. Lines of orange flame and smoke spat forth.

Lever, aim and fire! Lever, aim and fire!

The gun barrels grew hot with the continuous firing. And so it continued until all ten shots had been fired. After checking each man's set of targets, the announcement was made that only three shooters could pass through to the final round.

So, from a total of fifty shooters who had started,

only three were left.

Ben Fawlkner ran the Big Dipper, a small cattle spread situated some ten miles out of town. He was the oldest of the finalists. A thick mat of iron-grey hair, stiff and wiry, poked from beneath a well-worn Union Army hat. Fawlkner carried himself well. Tall and slim, he exuded a tough persona, tempered by the warmth of a smile that lit up the grizzled complexion.

In stark contrast, the next contestant had a mean, surly look. A livid scar reaching from his thin mouth to the tip of his left ear gave the jasper a permanent leer. Although no words were uttered, an irascible aura of menace issued a silent yet cogent threat to the other finalists.

Clean-shaven, Cabel Sharkey's intimidating posture boded ill-fortune to Gannon. He had discarded the challenge of Fawlkner. The old-timer didn't stand a chance. It was this other guy who was his main threat to coveting the prestigious Winchester.

Del held Sharkey's piercing gaze. A lazy half smile passed on the message that he was not intimidated in the least by the braggart's surly bluster. Had he known that the roughneck was none other than the killer of his buddy, Heaven knows what sparks would have flown.

As it was, both parties remained in ignorance of how close their destinies were interlinked.

A cough from the steward brought the trio's drifting attention back to the matter in hand. By this time, a large crowd had gathered, each person having paid a dollar to enjoy the performance.

'OK, boys,' the steward called, handing out fresh guns and a box of shells each. 'This is how it goes.' He paused to ensure that all three were paying full attention. 'Joe over yonder' – he indicated his partner at the end of the shooting range – 'will throw five small plates into the air. The man who smashes the most wins. Simple, ain't it? If one man drops behind, he is immediately eliminated. And in the event of a tie, Joe will continue until one of you misses. D'yuh all understand?'

Fawlkner and Del both nodded. Sharkey growled out, 'Cut the yappin', buster, and let's get on with it.'

The steward gave him a dirty frown but said nothing.

'Take up your weapons and load them,' he ordered solemnly. 'The first man to fire will be Ben Fawlkner.'

The rancher stepped forward to a round of applause.

'Just nod your head when you're ready for Joe to toss the plates.'

Fawlkner set his feet apart, a concentrated gleam in his pale-blue eyes. Then he gave a perceptible nod.

Five shots later he had hit four of the plates to a rip-snorting halloo of cheering. Ben was a popular guy in Borrego.

'Well done, Ben,' announced the steward. 'That's sure gonna be a hard target to beat. Next man forward.'

Sharkey stepped up to the line.

'Prepare to go home empty-handed, old man,' he snarled acidly. Fawlkner's shoulders tensed, his fists bunching. But he somehow managed to suppress the desire to wipe the smirk off the critter's leering puss.

Much as he silently implored the odious skunk to miss, there could be no denying that Cabel Sharkey was one helluva mean shot. He took down the five plates with practised ease.

Now it was Del's turn. He also managed five.

And so it went on for a further four plates each until finally, with his last shot . . . Sharkey missed.

The owlhoot cursed knowing that he'd been beaten. And it went down badly. A feral growl of anger hissed from between clenched teeth as he threw the empty gun to the ground. Swinging on his heel, he stamped off without a word to his adversary. Losing did not sit well on the thug's hunched shoulders. He needed a drink to drown out the crushing cheers for a worthy winner.

The sore loser was soon forgotten. Except by Ben Faulkner who openly spat out his contempt for the aggrieved runner-up.

'I sure don't object to being beaten by a better man,' the rancher observed loudly as he walked across to congratulate the winner. 'You call at my spread any time you're passing, Mr Gannon,' he enthused vigorously, shaking Del's hand. 'You'll be mighty welcome. The Big Dipper lies ten miles west of town. A sign points the way into the Anza valley. Yuh can't miss it.'

Del nodded his appreciation before mounting the rostrum to receive his prize.

Officiating at the presentation ceremony, Foxy Jim exuded an oily smile. It was as false as the diamond stick pin in his necktie. He made a grandiose speech extolling the winner's prowess before handing over the coveted prize which also included a brand new leather-tooled scabbard plus a box of special silver-tipped cartridges.

SEVEN

ELEPHANT BUTTE

With the cheers of the crowd ringing in his ears, Del was ushered towards the more permanent sector of Borrego. It was much like any other frontier settlement. Clapboard structures, some of which boasted ornately decorated cornices, were interspersed with others constructed of adobe and brick.

But there was something unusual about this place. For a moment he couldn't put his finger on it. Only when one of the accompanying throng shouted above the general hubbub did the penny drop.

'They've hired a new dancer at the Drago Palace. Let's go there.'

Howls of delight greeted this suggestion as they swung towards the garishly painted saloon.

That was it. Not only the Palace, but three other buildings also boasted the name of Drago. There was the Drago Theatre next door where the latest acts direct from San Francisco were advertised. And on the other side was the Drago Emporium, a general store that reputedly sold everything. The sign read *What we don't stock ain't worth buying.* And adjacent to that was Drago's Saddle and Tack Shop.

'Who's this guy Drago?' Del asked the man next to him.

'Jackson Drago runs the biggest ranch in the Anza Valley.' The guy didn't seem eager to extol the virtues of the rancher. 'Now he wants to take over the town as well. Rumour has it that he's set his sights on buying the *Borrego Tribune* then he'll be able to print anything that suits him.'

Del made no comment. Drago and his ambitions meant nothing to him.

Once inside the Palace Saloon, free drinks were pushed on to him. Every time he offered to pay the barman refused.

'I won't be taking no money from you tonight, mister,' he breezed, pushing another glass of finest Scotch whisky across the bar top. 'Seems like everybody wants to offer his congratulations with free drinks.'

Glasses of whisky were lined up like troopers on parade. Del's eyes were beginning to roll as more backslapping took place.

'Best shootin' I ever did see,' warbled one guy, sticking a cigar into Del's mouth and lighting it.

'Mind if we have another look at that special?' enquired another.

This was the third time that Del had been asked to

display his new rifle. He didn't mind; in fact, he was pleased at the unaccustomed attention.

'Sure thing, boys,' he drawled, his speech slow and slurred by the strong liquor. 'Just treat her the same as your wife.'

'That gun don't perform in bed as well, do it?' shot back one wit.

'It'll probably do a sight better job than you, Charley,' came an equally ribald response from his buddy.

Hoots of laughter all round as Del carefully removed the shiny new gun from its scabbard. Silence enveloped the gathering as the men all craned forward eager to touch the *One in a Thousand*.

But at the far end of the bar, one man was not in a felicitous frame of mind. Cabel Sharkey was becoming more irate as the level in the bottle he was nursing fell.

Peevish snorts of exasperation bubbled beneath the surface. That gun should have been his. Sharkey began mouthing excuses. Illogical reasons about having been cheated were festering in the gunman's warped brain.

By the time the bottle was empty, he had made up his mind. That gun was his of right. And he was going to have it. Shouldering off the bar, he pushed his way through the crowd on to the street outside.

Dark shadows of approaching night were spreading across land. One by one, twinkling oil lamps illuminated Borrego's main street. A plan was formulating that would ensure the accomplishment of his devious endeavour. The offer of hospitality made by the owner of the Big Dipper was the key. Too late now. But Sharkey could wait.

An evil grin split his coarse features as he grabbed hold of a young urchin rushing past.

'How'd yuh like to earn a silver dollar, kid?' He flipped the shiny coin up in the air which the boy stretched his hand out to catch. But Sharkey beat him to it. The outlaw guffawed at the kid's frustration. 'You can only have it when the iob has been done.'

The kid huffed some then shrugged resignedly. 'So what do I have to do?'

'There's a guy in the saloon who's just won a new rifle.' Sharkey pointed out Del through the front window. 'You tell him that Ben Fawlkner is inviting him to stay at his place while he's in the area. Make sure he knows that I had to get back to the ranch pronto but will expect him there tomorrow afternoon if'n he's agreeable to the notion.'

He waved the coin in front of the kid's gaping face. 'Only when I see that the message has been delivered can you have this.' Bulging eyes followed the tantalizing prize like a hovering snake. 'You got that?'

The boy nodded. 'Sure thing, Mr Fawlkner.'

Then he quickly disappeared through the door of the saloon and over to the bar. Sharkey, observing the conflab through the window, nodded his satisfaction when he saw the message being passed on. Then he waited on tenterhooks for the kid to return.

'Did he agree to my proposal?' asked the twitchy pretender.

The boy nodded. 'He'll be there, Mr Fawlkner.'

'Well done, kid,' he praised the boy. Flipping the shiny coin high into the air, the grubby urchin caught it with accomplished ease. He bit down to ensure it was genuine, then quickly disappeared down the adjoining alleyway.

Once again Sharkey peered through the window.

'See you tomorrow, *Mister* Gannon,' he smirked. 'Shame that you won't be seeing me. Fact is, you won't be seeing anything else . . . ever again.'

Then he also disappeared into the gloom.

Sharkey was in place well before the time that he expected his quarry to pass beneath the rocky overhang.

Elephant Butte made for a perfect spot to set up an ambush. The gnarled chunk of orange sandstone rose sheer from the rolling plain of saltbush and mesquite. Adjacent to the main trail serving southern California's town of San Felipe, its flat top gave the outlaw a sweeping panorama of the route that Del Gannon would have to follow.

The turn off for the Anza Valley and Fawlkner's Big Dipper spread lay a further two miles beyond.

Another hour passed before the bushwhacker saw the tell-tail sign of drifting dust rising into the dry air. He patted the stock of his Remington Rolling Block. A sturdy and reliable rifle, it had served him well over the years. Just the type of long gun to take out a man from this position atop the flat butte. But nothing compared to the *One in a Thousand* Winchester special, possession of which would soon pass to its rightful owner.

He settled down, sighting along the Remington's elongated barrel, following the unsuspecting rider as he drew ever closer.

Eyes narrowing to a focused squint, Sharkey wanted to make certain that he had the right target. At 200 yards he gave a snarl of delight. There was no mistaking that upright arrogant posture. And the object of his ambush could also be clearly seen.

The light tan of the new scabbard contrasted with the weathered saddle leathers. But best of all was what it contained.

With careful deliberation, the killer squeezed the trigger of the breech-loader.

'Nobody makes a fool out of Cabel Sharkey and lives to tell the tale,' he growled under his breath.

At 100 yards, the silence of the plain erupted to the single deep-throated roar of a the .50 calibre rifle. Sharkey's hard face split in a rabid grin as the rider tumbled from the saddle. Without further ado, he slid down a gully at the rear of the butte. Circling around to the front, he hurried across to the figure lying prone and unmoving on the sandy ground.

Offering barely a glance at the bleeding form, his only thought was to secure the all-important prize.

Displaying due reverence, he carefully removed the gun from its scabbard and gently caressed it like a newborn child. Bewitched eyes feasted upon the enchanting piece of hardware. But the moment of enthralment was cut short by a scream of anguish.

The killer's head jerked round.

Emerging from the far side of Elephant Butte was a twin-rigged buggy driven by a woman and escorted by a single rider. Sharkey drew his pistol and snapped off a couple of shots. They went wide but encouraged the intruders to haul rein and seek cover behind the buggy.

Sharkey had no wish to engage in a protracted gun battle. Other riders might not be far behind. Leaping on to the fallen man's horse, he dug in the spurs. The animal reared up on its hind legs at the unexpected jolt then galloped off across the plains. Shots from a carbine buzzed around his ears. Hugging the horse's neck, he escaped behind a cluster of boulders.

Risking a quick glance behind, he was pleased to note that the intruders had not taken up the pursuit.

The woman and her associate hurried over to the still body.

'Bring me some water and my medicine chest, Piecrust.' The soft yet assertive tone saw the older man touching his battered hat in respectful acknowledgement as he turn back towards the buggy.

It was fortuitous that Daisy Fawlkner had been on her monthly visit to Borrego to pick up some supplies for the ranch. Her father Ben had felt it wise to stay around the homestead owing to some recent trouble that had flared up with the largest spread in the Anza Valley.

Jackson Drago, owner of the Southern Cross, had offered to buy the Big Dipper but his generous if forceful proposition had been met with a blunt refusal. Drago had resented having his plan to take over the valley balked by this small-time interloper.

Used to getting his own way, words had been exchanged between the two men. Not exactly threats, but there was more than a hint of menace in the SC rancher's terse reaction.

Ben had not wanted his daughter making the trip to Borrego alone. He would have much preferred to do business in San Felipe. But the larger town was three days ride away. As a compromise, he had insisted that the ranch jack-of-all-trades should accompany her.

Piecrust Pete Warriner had acquired his sobriquet on account of the top rate quality of his culinary delights. The old-timer's cinammon and apple pie melted in the mouth. He was also pretty darned good at handling a branding iron and the myriad other jobs that a working ranch demanded.

Daisy, however, had an ulterior motive for visiting Borrego. She wanted to pick up some material that had been on order at the dressmaker's shop for two months. The coincidence of the duo turning up at that particular moment had saved Del Gannon's life. Had the killer been accorded more time to linger, he would doubtless have finished the job properly.

'You keep a sharp eye open in case that varmint decides to come back, Piecrust,' said the girl, 'while I get to work on this fella.'

A grunt of pain issued from the injured man's twisted mouth.

'He's still alive!'

The exclamation found the old guy hurrying back with the wherewithal to staunch the flow of blood.

'Good job we turned up when we did,' he remarked, moving away to take up sentry duty.

Del tried to raise himself but fell back.

'Easy there, mister,' urged the girl as she skilfully cleaned and bandaged the shoulder wound. 'You're durned lucky the bullet went right through. And it ain't broken no bones neither.'

Del's eyes flickered open. All he could see was a cascade of golden locks encasing a serenely calm face.

'My angel of mercy,' he croaked. A shiver rippled through the muscular torso before he lost consciousness. Daisy continued with her ministrations while studying the ruggedly handsome profile. Her face assumed a guilty blush at the sensual thoughts swimming around inside her head. What was she thinking? Although there was no denying, he sure was pleasing on the eye.

Shaking off the carnal reflections, she called across to her associate.

'Give me a hand over here, Piecrust. We need to get him into the buggy and back to the ranch lickety-split.'

Musing silently to herself as she packed away her things, the girl idly speculated as to the reasoning behind the ambush.

Warriner appeared to read her mind.

'This fella must have ruffled somebody's feathers to get himself ambushed out here.'

The comment brought a thoughtful nod of agreement from the girl. 'Like as not he'll let us know in his own good time.'

Hauling the team around, they headed back for the Big Dipper.

The bushwhacker's horse which had been found behind the butte trotted aimiably behind. The animal seemed unperturbed at having lost its previous owner. Sharkey's rough handling would not be missed.

An hour later they pulled into the yard fronting the primitive log ranch house. Ben Fawlkner was there to greet them, a frown of concern etched across his grizzled face.

'I didn't expect you two back until this evening,' intoned the concerned rancher stepping down off the covered veranda to greet his kin. 'Some'n serious must have happened to bring you back early.'

'You could say that, boss,' replied Warriner drawing the buggy to a halt. His thumb signalled for the rancher to look in the back.

'What in tarnation. . . ?'

The startled ejaculation elicited a fretful response from his daughter who leapt off the buggy.

'Time for explanations later, Pa. Help me get him inside.'

All three gently carried the injured man inside the house and laid him on the bed in the spare room at the rear.

Only when more permanent attention to the injury had been administered did the girl relate the incident. The bullet wound had required several stitches. Not that there was a great deal to tell. That would have to wait until their guest was fit and able to assuage their curiosity.

The unwritten code of the West was not to press a man about his business. Hospitality was unconditional. If a man chose not to reveal his circumstances, they would respect his silence. Although in this case when a man had been shot from ambush, keeping close-mouthed might prove difficult to maintain.

It was another week before Del was finally allowed to get up.

His nurse had been firm in her determination to ensure that her patient did not have a relapse. During the period of his illness, he had slipped in and out of consciousness on numerous occasions. Only Daisy's constant ministering had prevented the fever from taking a firm hold.

The wound in his shoulder was stiff and sore. He was just glad that it was his left side that was affected. That meant his gun hand was free to execute his own brand of attention when the time came, which it surely would.

For the first time, he could now observe the ministering angel who had brought him back from the brink. And she was a sight to behold. Del Gannon was lost for words. Unused to such dealings, he could only mumble his thanks. The girl accepted the reserve of her patient with modest decorum.

'I'll leave you to get dressed while I see how Piecrust is getting on with the midday meal.'

Del's face crinkled in puzzlement.

The girl's laugh lit up the room. 'Piecrust Pete Warriner.' Her delicate mouth opened revealing teeth whiter than the winter snows. 'The old reprobate was chaperoning me to Borrego when we disturbed that bushwhacker. He used to be Pa's old sergeant. They were together all through the war and have stuck with each other ever since. It was me who gave Pete the nickname due to him being a dab hand in the kitchen, as you'll soon find out.'

That was when Del realized how hungry he was. But, more important, all he was wearing was a nightshirt.

'Was it you that. . . ?' The question remained unfinished as he vaguely indicated his lack of clothing.

'Someone had to get you out of those bloodstained duds.' Then with a coquettish wink, she left the room leaving the man gaping at the closed door.

Ten minutes later, Warriner appeared with some fresh range gear for Del to wear. 'Your other duds weren't worth cleaning up,' he said, laying the garments down on the bed. 'You and me are about the same size so I've dug you out some spares. Hope you have a healthy appetite.' The old soldier sniffed the air. 'Steak pie, potatoes and green beans suit you?'

'Sounds good to me, Piecrust,' he replied, his mouth watering. 'And much obliged for the gear. Pity about my other stuff. I bought the pants and shirt brand new in Superstition after selling my old Henry.'

'They sure didn't smell new,' was the acrid rejoinder.

Del was about to pass a suitable riposte when the sound of hoofs drew their attention to the open window.

A half-dozen riders had galloped into the yard. They slammed to a juddering halt in front of the homestead. Ben Fawlkner had seen their dust and was waiting on the veranda, a Sharps Big .50 clutched to his chest.

'What do you want, Drago!' The demand was brusquely delivered.

A stocky figure around the same age and sporting a thick black moustache nudged his large bay forward. 'You know darned well what I want, Fawlkner. You gonna accept my terms for this land?'

'I gave you my answer last time,' snapped the rancher. 'Nothing has changed. The Big Dipper ain't for sale.'

'You're a danged fool, mister,' the other man chided. 'My offer is a good one. You won't get better elsewhere. This is your last chance.'

'Are you threatening me?' snarled Fawlkner taking a step forward.

'Take it anyway you want.' The Southern Cross rancher paused, leaning forward across the bay's neck. His rejoinder was measured and tersely conveyed, a menacing utterance that left no room for doubt. 'But one way or another, I intend to have this land.'

Before Fawlkner had chance to react, another rider pushed through from behind. 'You want me to finalize this deal with a bullet, Mr Drago?'

'No need for that, Cabel,' said the rancher. An evil smile revealed the yellow teeth of a baccy chewer. He expectorated into the dust at his adversary's feet. 'Not yet anyways. I'm sure that Mr Fawlkner here will see sense once he comes to realize the futility of holding out on me.'

Back in the spare room, Del had recognized the chestnut and the man riding him. This varmint had to be the bastard who had gunned him down.

Irate features flushed with indignation. He was all for dashing outside and confronting the skunk there and then. Only the restraining hands of Piecrust Pete prevented what was a futile gesture doomed to failure with the end result being his own permanent demise.

'Hold on there, Del,' declared the ranch hand, tightening his grip. 'There are six heavily armed jaspers out there just itching to haul off. All it would take is one false move and the boss would be cut down.'

Gannon struggled against the firm grip. All he could see was the lowdown rat who had robbed him of the special Winchester and would have killed him for sure had not Piecrust and the girl happened along when they did. Nothing else mattered. An all-consuming anger contaminated his soul.

But the ex-bronc rider's body was still very much weakened.

The older man continued to hold him in a grip of steel, urging reason. And slowly, the logic of Warriner's argument began to filter through the red mist of hate.

'When you're fully recovered, then you can choose the time and place to get even,' murmured the persuasive voice in his ear. 'And believe me, son, this ain't it.'

Del nodded his understanding. His body relaxed. 'Guess you're right, Pete. I just saw red knowing the skunk was out there. Thanks a bunch for bringing me to my senses.'

Outside, Drago hauled the bay around.

'OK, boys, let's go.' Then to Fawlkner he added, 'Next time I come back this way, it'll be with a bill of sale. And you better be prepared to sign on the dotted line.'

Sharkey led the way across the front yard deliberately trampling down the vegetable patch that Daisy had been cultivating. With a loud yahoo, the man then drew his pistol and shot one of the chickens.

Hoots of ecstatic derision greeted the brutal action as the Southern Cross riders galloped off.

EIGHT

LEGEND OF THE STONES

It was a somewhat chastened Ben Fawlkner who returned to the house. Nothing was said as he tried to figure out what the best course of action ought to be following Jackson Drago's implied threat.

Del Gannon was only a temporary resident of the Big Dipper, but already he felt beholden to the rancher and his daughter, not to mention old Piecrust Warriner. Knowing the identity of the pesky varmint who had attempted to kill him, and that he was employed by Fawlkner's rival, had suddenly made things personal.

The rancher's problems were now his.

Del tried unsuccessfully to convince himself that the presence of the delectable Daisy Fawlkner had nothing to do with his decision to hang around in support of the Big Dipper against its bullying neighbour.

'I'm with you all the way, Pa,' snapped the girl, clenching her fists. 'No way are we going to give in to Drago and his bullyboy tactics.'

But the old rancher was having second thoughts. He suddenly felt every one of his fifty-five years. The broad shoulders slumped.

'I don't know,' he wavered. 'Drago is holding all the aces. The Southern Cross is a much bigger spread than ours. And now he's gone and hired himself some outside help. That hard-ass riding the chestnut was a gunslinger if ever I saw one.'

'You're right there, Ben,' agreed Del. 'That's my cayuse. And the rider is the skunk who gunned me down. It was only Pete's persuasive manner that stopped me getting my head blown off.' He winked at the old soldier. 'I was so darned mad on seeing him out there, my mind went blank.'

'You can't surrender to domineering tyrants like Drago, Pa,' cut in Daisy with vigour. Her cheeks flushed red with indignation, the fiery gaze fiercely intense and challenging. 'And I can handle a rifle as good as any man.' Her slim figure stiffened as she dared her father to deny the claim.

'The gal is sure right there, boss,' concurred old Piecrust.

'And don't forget me, Ben,' added Del. 'This is my business just as much as it is your'n. If'n it wasn't afore, it sure is now. That gunslick is toting the hardware I won fair and square, and is riding my horse.

Before I'm through, he'll also be carrying my lead in his belly.'

Once the initial zeal for a fight had settled down, the true nature of their task became clear. Four against a much larger spread which now had a hired gunman for back-up were not good odds.

A tense atmosphere of thoughtful deliberation settled over the quartet as they resumed their interrupted meal in silence.

It was Del who spoke first.

'My reckoning is that Drago will give you a spell to consider his offer again before making another move.'

'That was my feeling as well,' agreed Fawlkner pushing a lump of beef around his plate.

'In the meantime, perhaps Daisy could show me around your place.' He threw a hopeful glance at the girl. 'Help me to get my bearings.'

Daisy's eyes lit up. 'We'll head out soon as I've tidied myself up.'

Del didn't think she could look any more delectable. His doe-eyed gaze went unnoticed.

'It ain't a large spread,' said Fawlkner. 'And much of what I do own is scrub land.'

'Only the western range has enough grass to carry our cattle,' Piecrust butted in, while clearing away the dishes.

He scratched the back of his head screwing the wizened mask of his face into a manic contortion. The bizarre manoeuvre always brought a hoot of laughter from Daisy who clapped her hands in glee.

Piecrust's less than handsome visage twisted all the more. He enjoyed the young girl's attention, envying his buddy the daughter that he never had. However, being a surrogate uncle came a close second.

But the old guy's face pulling was not meant as an attempt at levity.

Fawlkner caught on to his sidekick's unease.

'Some'n bothering you, old buddy?'

'I just can't figure out why a big shot like Drago should want to take over the Big Dipper.' The crinkled face twisted in the opposite direction. But this time, it evoked no hilarity. 'Grass for running a few steers? Even the few wells we have are barely enough to water the squash and melon crops. Most of the land is pretty barren. Drago is holding all the best land at his end of the valley.'

Bafflement replaced the awkward grimace.

Daisy and her father were equally nonplussed.

'Maybe following this conducted tour,' Del propounded, eyeing the girl with a suggestive regard, 'I can offer a fresh outlook on the problem. See things from a different angle.'

'Sure can't hurt none,' agreed Fawlkner.

'Then let's get saddled up,' cut in the girl, leaping to her feet. 'Ain't no time like the present.'

By early afternoon they had ventured over to the eastern edge of the holding. This section was close to the start of the desert. Bleak and remote, it was too arid and infertile for raising either animals or crops.

'This is the first time I've ever been this far east,' Daisy announced, wrinkling her nose at sight of the austere terrain. 'Another couple of miles and it'll be pure sand and rock.'

They rode on across the desiccated landscape where nought but barrel cacti, catclaw and saltbush vied for dominance with the ubiquitous mesquite.

'No point going any further,' said Daisy reining up. 'There's nothing out here to interest a landgrabber like Jackson Drago.'

'Guess you're right at that,' Del concurred. Although he was still not satisfied, he inclined to the notion that the answer was staring him in the face.

Narrowed eyes avidly scanned the sandy ground, hoping that something would trigger a thought.

That was when he saw it.

Only the angle of the sun at that precise moment made it visible to the naked eye. Then it was gone. But that split second had revealed a shiny black disk of stone. Quickly he stepped down reaching for the elusive chimera. Delving on hands and knees, his questing hands discovered more of the same.

'What is it, Del?' asked the bewildered girl. 'The sun getting to you? Maybe we should head back for you to take a nap.'

Ignoring the puzzled queries, he stood up and showed his finding to the girl. 'Have you ever seen chunks of rock like these before?'

A baffled shake of the head followed as she peered down at the stones. Del fished out the bag given to him by the Yuma chieftain, Painted Tail. The comparison left him in no doubt that they were the same type. Was this the original source of the black stones?

And if so, what did they mean?

Seeing the girl's sceptical regard as to his sanity, Del quickly filled her in on his adventures with the Indians. He also told her of his plans to run an orange farm in the San Joaquin Valley.

'I have a feeling that there is more to these stones than meets the eye,' he proposed thoughtfully. 'Drago must have also come across them and figured out their importance.'

'I can't see what value there is in a few Indian good luck charms.' Daisy's remark was less than positive.

'Well there ain't nothing else that I can see that explains his interest in the Big Dipper.' Del swung his horse around and spurred off back in the direction of the ranch. His decidedly dubious escort followed.

No further words were spoken until they arrived back at the house.

'Any luck?' asked Fawlkner, who was busy cleaning and oiling all the guns in his possession.

Without any preamble, the Texan leapt off his horse and handed the black stones to his host.

'You ever seen stones like these before, Ben?'

The older man sensed the excitement in his guest's tremulous voice. Quickly he examined them. A look of wonder spread across his weathered face. 'Where in thunder did you come across these?'

His passionate zeal piqued the girl's curiosity. 'You know something about them, Pa?'

'Never seen 'em afore,' he claimed rolling the mysterious chunks in his big gnarled hand. 'But there's an old legend I was told about these black stones. Just another tale from the desert . . . or so I thought.'

'You gonna fill us in, boss?' Piecrust Warriner voiced the eagerness of the other two.

'Come inside and we'll crack a new jug of moonshine,' said Fawlkner leading the way. 'Then I'll tell you about the story of Pegleg Smith.'

The rancher had heard the legend from an old prospector.

The story began back in 1829 when Pegleg had gone beaver trapping with some partners along the Colorado River. The haul had been much better than expected. So the leader of the party decided to send old Pegleg ahead to Santa Fe to sell half of their hides.

But Pegleg was a wily cove and saw an opportunity to make more by selling them to Yankee clipper traders along the Pacific Coast. And by doing that, all the profits would not have to be shared with the other six trappers.

The journey from Yuma to the coast was hazardous and no more than a handful had attempted it at that time. The Mojave Desert to the north had been crossed but the Indians had proved to be as much a problem as the sandy wasteland. Pegleg, therefore, decided to take the southerly route where he knew the Yuma Indians were more amenable.

By packing plenty of water he should be able to reach the far side without any difficulty.

All went well for the first few days. Then he hit the

notorious Algodones Dunes. The pack mule soon got bogged down in the endlessly soft sand. To compound Pegleg's difficulties, a sand storm blew up that lasted for five days causing an unforeseen delay. Not only that: with no maps, signs or landmarks to guide him, progress slowed to a snail's pace.

The greedy trapper soon realized that he would have to ditch some of the valuable pelts if he were to survive the crossing of the treacherous wilderness. It was too late regretting his rash decision to cheat on his buddies: the die had been cast. He had gone too far now to turn back.

Eventually he reached the Salton Sink. But that flat expanse of white salt proved to be equally daunting. Water was running desperately low. One of the pack mules collapsed from exhaustion which meant that its load had to be abandoned. Struggling onward towards the setting sun, Pegleg crawled to the top of a low hill to try and get a better look at the terrain.

And that was where he discovered the black stones.

Not according them any particular significance, he nonetheless pocketed a handful. Then promptly forgot all about them. His priority at that moment was pure survival.

The rancher paused in his enthralling narration to lubricate his tonsils. His audience remained mesmerized by the exciting myth that had suddenly become very real and personal to them.

Del chose the lull to pose a question. 'So that must

have been on Big Dipper land?'

'Sure seems the case,' agreed Fawlkner stoking up his corncob pipe. 'Just like you, Pegleg had managed to cross the infamous California Desert. But he was left with only half his original supply of pelts. He eventually sold them in Los Angeles. Nobody knows when he finally discovered the true value of the black stones.'

This was what they all wanted to know. What exactly were these black stones that had been unearthed?

There was a pause as they all stared at the mysterious discovery.

Then the rancher turned to Del. 'I guess you never bothered to check out those stones you were given, because if'n you had, the truth would have been revealed.'

Del toyed with the stones, silently willing the older man to continue.

Fawlkner slowly picked up a knife and began scraping at the hard black surface of a stone. Acute tension crackled like dry leaves as the watchers anxiously peered down as the outer covering was peeled away.

And there it was. The yellow gleam that had drawn the eyes of greedy men throughout history.

Del grabbed another of the stones and hurriedly chipped away. The same mesmeric allure assaulted his gaping peepers. He felt like cheering, dancing a jig. But was it just a myth? A cruel jest played by nature to trick the unwary? Could it really be . . . *gold?*

His eyes lifted, seeking reassurance from the story-teller.

'Most folks were disbelieving,' the rancher went on. 'Rumours circulated that Pegleg Smith had come back this way some years later to try to locate the source of his black gold. But he never did find the spot.' Fawlkner's ardent gaze fastened on to that of his quest. 'But it seems like you have, Del.'

It was Piecrust Warriner who brought the excited thoughts of the gathering back to earth with a bump.

'And it looks as though Drago has done the same.'

The euphoric atmosphere of moments before had been burst like a balloon. A morose silence enveloped the room as the grim consequences of the discovery churned around in their minds.

'So now we know the reason he wants to get his grubby hands on the Big Dipper,' murmured Fawlkner bunching his fists. 'His boys must have been checking out the east range for maverick steers and come across them by accident.'

Del examined the stones a little closer. 'My figuring is that he's had them checked out by an assayer and they have been passed as the genuine article. Otherwise why bother to get his mitts on the land.'

Fawlkner grimly nodded his agreement.

'I ain't never heard of black gold afore, boss,' remarked a puzzled Pete Warriner rolling the heavy nuggets around in his hand. 'What exactly makes it like this?'

'From what I heard,' the rancher explained, 'the gold is mixed with copper and its the passage of time that has given it that black crusty sheen.'

'Easy to just pass them off as worthless chunks if'n you don't know the legend,' added Daisy.

'Now that we know Drago's real intentions,' Fawlkner stated in a sombre voice, 'anybody got any ideas as to how we play it from here on?'

'First off,' declared his daughter, 'we will also have to get these stones assayed to make certain they are the real stuff. I'll head for town first thing in the morning. Sooner we learn the truth, the better.'

'You ain't going alone,' asserted Ben Fawlkner firmly. 'Look what happened the last time.'

'That bushwhacker wasn't after me,' countered Daisy. 'I've done that trip a thousand times and more with no problems. It was mere coincidence that we happened to be passing at the right moment to save Del's hide.'

The stubborn streak gleaned from her mother's side of the family was reflected in the starchy expression.

May Fawlkner had died two years before from the fever. She was buried on a low hillock behind the ranch house. A small well-tended grave site had been made in the shade of some cottonwoods. Ben had made it his business to visit the grave each evening for a few quiet words with his wife.

It was one more reason why the girl was so disturbed when her father had hinted at selling up under pressure.

'In any case, you boys will be needed around here just in case Drago makes an early move to force the issue,' she added with a decisive shake of her flaxen hair.

No amount of cajoling would persuade the girl to accept an escort.

Del in particular was disappointed.

He would have liked some time alone to get better acquainted with this feisty she-wolf. Still, there would be plenty of time for that now he had chosen to stick around.

NINE

KIDNAPPED

Daisy set off for Borrego early the next morning.

Approaching the lone sentinel of Elephant Butte she was surprised to see three riders emerge from behind the hunk of gnarled rock. A ripple of trepidation trickled down her spine. She drew her horse to a stop as the riders jogged forward. A quick glance behind confirmed that her alarm was well founded. Two more were blocking any chance of escape.

As they drew closer, the grinning face of Cabel Sharkey swam into focus.

'You're on the trail mighty early, miss,' he growled, leaning forward and running a lustful eye over the comely form. 'A mite too early I'd say. Now I wonder why that could be?'

The question raised a few snickers from his associates.

'Maybe we ought to frisk her?' suggested a Mexican wrangler known as Ventana. A libidinous gaze said he had more in mind than a mere search.

'You go ahead, Ventana,' said Sharkey. 'Me and the boys will just sit and watch, just to make sure you do the job properly.' More guffaws followed as the leering cowpoke stepped down.

Although shaken by this unexpected turn of events, Daisy was not about to surrender willingly. A left hand dug out her rifle from its scabbard. Levering a round into the barrel, she swung it towards the Mexican.

The sudden move caught the assailants by surprise. They had not expected any form of serious resistance from the girl.

It was Sharkey who reacted first. Palming his revolver, the hired gunman snapped off a shot that smashed into the stock of the rifle before it could be fired. Splinters of wood flew in all directions.

The jolting force of the impact sent the girl head over heels off the back of her horse. She landed with a dull thump on the hard ground.

Luckily it was only her pride that was injured. Stumbling to her feet, she brushed herself down and nervously faced the ring of grinning men who now surrounded her.

'Seems like we got us a real firebrand here, boys,' observed the oldest of the bushwackers. 'Check her out careful like to make sure there ain't no derringer lurking inside that feisty frame.'

'Be glad to, Isaac,' replied Ventana moving

forward. His drooping moustache twitched with unsuppressed ardour. The girl backed away, the blood draining from her face.

Isaac Hayes had been with Drago a long time. Dark rings beneath the hooded eyes spoke of hard times past punching cows for a living. He was the foreman and had no intention of seeing the girl mistreated. His boss had other plans for her.

'Don't worry, girl,' he said in a reassuring yet firm tone. 'We ain't gonna harm you. The boys are only having a bit of fun.' His pointed gaze bit into the grinning wrangler effectively removing the lascivious drool from the Mexican's paunchy face. The leathery features looked as if they had been carved with a blunt knife. 'Ain't that right, Ventana?'

The rotund greaser speared the foreman with a malevolent look. Hayes leaned forward defying him to ignore the order. Ventana hesitated, peering at the faces of the other riders. All wore blank expressions. There was no support there. Hayes was well respected and not a jasper to be bucked.

He shrugged, then proceeded to roughly pat the girl down, although he still couldn't resist a brief mauling of the shapely contours. Daisy's features remained cold and deadpan throughout the humiliating experience.

'All clear!' he grunted morosely returning to his horse.

After helping Daisy remount her own horse, the foreman swung around and led the way back over the foothills in the direction of the Southern Cross. Daisy remained hemmed into the middle of the group throughout.

Her abduction had been well planned.

Drago had posted lookouts at strategic points overlooking the Big Dipper ranch buildings. The sentinels were given strict orders to observe any suspicious movements only. No attempt to intervene was to be made.

It was the visit of Gannon and the girl to the eastern range that had perturbed Drago. And when it was reported that the man had shown undue interest in a particular locale, Drago felt obliged to act. He knew that like himself, Fawlkner would want to verify his discovery.

By abducting the one person Ben Fawlkner held dearer than life itself, Drago knew that he held a winning hand. His adversary would do anything to get his daughter back unscathed. Signing over the Big Dipper would then become a formality.

But the devious critter had to act quickly. Hence a surreptitious watch over the Fawlkner homestead. And it had paid off.

A purpling sky shot through with streaks of orange and pink blazed across the western backdrop. The sun had long since disappeared below the serrated ramparts of the mountains from where the guardian of night now stalked across the land.

Piecrust Warriner applied a lighted taper to the oil lamps in the cabin.

For the third time in the last half-hour, Ben

Fawlkner peered at his watch. He was becoming restive. Lines of worry ribbed his forehead. Voicing his thoughts out loud, he grumbled, 'Daisy should have been back by now. Goldarn it! Picking up some material don't take this long. And she also had to see to the verification of the stones.'

'Fixing up an assay takes time, boss.' The old cook spooned out a plateful of his son-of-a-gun stew. He was also concerned for the girl's safety. But he tried to reassure his old buddy in the pacifying manner to which the rancher usually responded. 'And, like as not, she could have stayed over at Rachel Kenyon's. Once them gals get down to needle and thread talk, there ain't no stoppin' them.'

Fawlkner muttered something under his breath.

'Pete's right,' Del agreed. 'No sense getting all fired up. Daisy is a smart cookie. She's like all women. They lose track of time once they get to prattling with each other. She must have realized too late that she couldn't get back here afore dark.'

That appeared to satisfy the rancher who dipped a hunk of bread into the tasty concoction.

Before the three men had time to settle down to eat their evening meal, the uneasy silence was shattered by a harsh crack. The front window shattered. Glass spewed across the room. The rock that had caused the damage struck the earthen bowl containing the stew, splattering hot food across the table.

Caught completely off guard, the diners tumbled back off their chairs on to the plank floor.

Del Gannon was the first to recover.

Drawing his revolver, he hurried across to the broken window and peered out into the darkness. All he saw was the brief silhouette of a horse and rider disappearing into the stygian gloom. A couple of shots whistled after the attacker. But neither hit their mark.

'What in thunder was that all about?' growled a startled Ben Fawlkner scrambling to his feet.

'Looks like somebody had a message to pass on,' observed Piecrust, retrieving the rock which had a piece of paper tied to it. He handed it to his boss.

Fawlkner eyed the grubby note, concern etched across his ashen features. He swallowed nervously. 'Ain't no prizes for guessing who this is from.' The croaking remark stuck in his throat. 'You read it,' he said passing the note to Gannon. 'I've got me a bad feeling about this.'

The Texan was no less anxious. Nervously he read the message, mouthing the contents to himself.

'Well?' snapped the waspish voice of the rancher. 'No point keeping us in suspense. What does that bastard Drago want?' Tears welled in the old guy's eyes. 'He's got Daisy, ain't he?' But he already knew the answer.

It was Del's turned to feel awkward. Drawing in a lungful of air, he narrated the missive exactly as it was written.

Fawlkner I have your daughter. If you want her back in one piece, you'll sign over the Big Dipper to me. Don't try any funny business or the girl dies. You have forty-eight hours to decide.

It wasn't signed.

'Drago obviously doesn't want his name attached to any threatening notes.' Del spat out the observation with venom. He passed the note to Fawlkner whose face was blank, the eyes glassy and bloodshot. His shoulders slumped.

'That's it then,' he muttered dolefully. 'He's won. There ain't no way I can put Daisy's life in danger. She's worth more'n a few measly hunks of black gold.'

Del remained silent. He was of the same view. But he was not ready to surrender without considering all the options. He stood up and lit a stogie. Drawing the smoke deep into his lungs, he moved over to the door and went outside into the still of the night. He needed time to think.

Overhead, a myriad tiny pinpricks of light twinkled. A constant and unvarying tableau immune to the vagaries of the human tragedy unfolding below. Gazing up at the mesmeric blanket helped to concentrate the mind, bring the traumatic events into focus. And thus slowly a plan of action began to form in Del's mind.

Fifteen minutes later, he re-entered the cabin.

His mouth was set in a thin line of determination. Fawlkner had not moved during the brief period of his absence. The rancher just sat and stared at the floor. Del gritted his teeth. He knew that the old guy was on the verge of despair. And who wouldn't be having received such dire tidings?

He slanted a wary eye at the rancher steeling himself to declare his plan.

A brief cough elicited no reaction from the distraught man. Del gestured to the waiting Piecrust indicating for him to try breaking into the mood of despondency that had enveloped his old comrade in arms.

Warriner sensed that the Texan had something up his sleeve.

He began busying himself to tidy the mess caused by the rock. Uncorking a bottle of hooch, he poured a glass and pushed it into Fawlkner's hand.

'A drink might ease the pain, boss,' he whispered gingerly.

The rancher took a large gulp. A spate of coughing occasioned by the harsh liquor appeared to break the spell giving Piecrust the opportunity to intervene. 'Del has some'n on his mind,' he said.

Slowly the bloodshot eyes swung towards his guest.

Without any further preamble, Del launched into the details of his plan. It was bold and brazen. A daring strike at the heart of the enemy's holdings.

When he had finished, a grain of colour had returned to the pale face of the rancher. He took another drink of the moonshine, this time savouring the flavour. The benumbed pallor of minutes previously had dissolved. A fresh interest in life had returned.

'You reckon it will work?' The query was hesitant, tentative, still lacking conviction. 'Ain't no doubt that what you're proposing will put a burr up Drago's ass. But anything that puts my gal's life in danger ain't for considering.'

Del raised an eyebrow, his hands splayed in surrender. 'There's always gonna be some risk to any plan.' Then he held the worried rancher with a stoical regard. 'But just ask yourself this, Ben: would Daisy have wanted her pa to back down to this rat? My figuring is that she would want us to try anything to foil his rotten game.'

'I agree with Del, boss,' Piecrust interjected with vigour. 'Daisy sure wouldn't want her pa surrendering without a fight.'

The old rancher nodded. 'Guess you're right, boys,' he concurred. 'At first light we'll set things in motion. That skunk is gonna regret the day he tangled with Ben Fawlkner.'

TEN

A BURNING ISSUE

Early the next morning, a light shone through the broken front window of the Big Dipper ranch house. It was still dark. On the eastern horizon, a faint tinge of yellow heralded the approach of dawn.

Inside the cabin, the three avengers went about their business in silence. A tense atmosphere hung over the room as weapons were checked and fresh ammunition was packed. This was going to be a make-or-break situation.

Fawlkner was the most nervous of the three.

It was his daughter's life that was on the line. The plan proposed by Gannon had considerable merit. But like all such schemes, there was much that could go wrong.

Yet try as he might, the rancher could not figure out any viable alternative. Short of full capitulation, which meant handing over his entire holding to the thieving critter, there did not appear to be any other choice. And even then, a low-life such as Drago could easily decide to get rid of any troublemakers left who could cause him problems with the authorities.

The ageing rancher's shoulders squared off. A glint of iron determination was evident in his stiff posture.

'Time to go, boys,' he said finishing a mug of coffee and standing up. The directive was self-assured, brimful of confidence. It had to be. There was no going back once they left the ranch.

The false dawn had opened up a window of light across the Vallecito Mountains by the time the trio of riders had reached the main connecting trail between San Felipe and Borrego. It was here that they parted company. Hands were shaken, final affirmations expressed as to each man's allotted task.

'Bring her back safe, Del. I'm counting on you.' A catch in Fawlkner's throat betrayed the tension racking his sturdy frame.

The tall Texan merely nodded. Now that the die had been cast, the plan in which he had so assiduously believed seemed full of holes. But any doubts he harboured were hidden behind an impassive mask of certitude. This was no time for vacillating.

Nudging his horse into motion, he headed off across the flats in the direction of the Southern Cross. His two associates continued along the well-worn trail towards Borrego. Each of them was leading a fully laden mule. Few words were passed by the two men.

Twice they were forced to pull off the trail into hiding.

The early morning stagecoach was the first to rumbled past barely more than a stone's throw from their place of concealment in a cluster of trees. Another half-hour passed when they had to avoid a mule train. On both occasions they were fortunate to have sufficient means of concealment. But that sort of luck could not last.

The final section of the journey was across a bleak plain covered in waist-high sagebrush and prickly pear, OK for men to hide in but not the horses. To maintain their clandestine position, Fawlkner judged it prudent for them to leave the main trail. It would take longer to reach Borrego, but their secrecy would then be assured.

For what they intended doing, it was imperative that no connection to the impending action should fall on anybody from the Big Dipper.

The tension was palable as they drew ever closer to their destination. Nerve endings twanged like banjo strings. Reaching the western edge of the town, a copse of trees provided cover to observe the settlement. Dismounting, the horses were secured in readiness for a quick getaway.

It was still early. Few people would be about yet awhile, so there would be nobody to disturb their nefarious endeavour.

The rancher was loath to carry out such a drastic course of action. But this was the only way to lure Jackson Drago and his men away from the Southern

Cross spread so that Del Gannon could do his bit.

Lined up below were the inert victims of their attack. Wooden buildings, four of which were owned by the devious critter and would soon be consigned to oblivion.

Fire was a major fear of all western townships where wood was the primary means of construction. Fawlkner was glad that they were all together which meant less chance of the fire spreading to other parts of the town.

'I'll start at the far end,' he stated. 'Give me ten minutes to get in position before you get the first blaze started. That's the saddle shop. If all goes to plan, we should meet in the middle at the Palace. But if not, we'll meet back here. You remember the drill?'

Warriner's narrowed gaze was fixed on the tinder-dry structures as he made to reply. 'Set the fused sticks in rags pushed beneath the back wall.' The oil-soaked rags were intended to spread the conflagration at a much faster rate following the explosions. 'Don't worry. I know the score, boss.' Taut nerves lent the brusque retort a slur of irritation that was alien to the ranch hand's inherent good nature.

Fawlkner understood and let it pass.

Two hessian sacks were slung on either side of the mule. One contained bottles of highly combustible oil, the other held three lengths of fuse wire attached to sticks of dynamite, each calculated for a one-minute burn.

There would not be any time for delays if they were to escape unscathed.

When Gannon had first mooted his plan, the notion of setting fire to Drago's properties had been received with scepticism by Ben Fawlkner.

Piecrust Pete, however, supported the notion. And it was he who had suggested the use of delayed fuses controlled by lighted candle stubs.

'And it just so happens that I have some in my box of tricks,' he had declared with a flourish, extracting the said items from a tool chest. 'They were to be used for blasting out those deep-rooted tree stumps in the yard.'

Del's eyes lit up. 'Does that mean you also have some sticks of dynamite to go with them?'

'Sure does,' smirked the old soldier. 'And I know how to use 'em'n all.'

'Piecrust here doubled as an explosives expert during the war,' said Fawlkner. The clear praise for his old sergeant's proficiency yielded a wide grin of appreciation on the gnarled features. 'This old-timer was the first guy to figure out the use of delayed explosions using fuse wire and candles. A heap of enemy installations suffered badly due to his expertise. And the system allowed us to get far away before they blew up.'

Fawlkner swallowed nervously. But now the time for action had arrived, he felt loath to destroy sections of the town. The fires could quite easily spread to adjacent structures run by innocent people, many of whom were held to be good friends.

Again doubts began to surface.

Should he have succumbed to Drago's threats? Accepted his offer? It was pretty generous considering.

Then the worry lines around his mouth tightened. What evidence was there that the crooked varmint would keep his promise to release the girl? Fawlkner struggled to persuade himself that the double-dealing rancher would not want anybody left around to cause trouble once he had acquired the valuable land. Himself included.

Yet still the doubts persisted. After all, his daughter's life was at stake here.

It was the firm yet decisive interjection of his sidekick cutting into the morbid cogitations which brought the rancher back from the brink.

'You OK, boss?' Piecrust couldn't help noticing the grey palor clouding the rancher's face.

'Y-yeah, sure, old buddy,' muttered Fawlkner visibly shaking off the devil sitting on his shoulder. 'Just some last-minute nerves. I'm fine now.'

'Time to go then?'

Fawlkner responded with a curt nod, watching as his old sergeant heaved the laden backpack over his shoulder. His gaze followed the old-timer down a slope and into the amalgam of shacks crammed behind the main street. As soon as Warriner was out of sight, he hustled down the slope aiming towards the left where his own first objective was located.

Daylight was struggling to make its presence felt. Thick banks of dark cloud brushed the tops of the enclosing hills blotting out the new day's sun. A flash storm was brewing. The extra gloom was certainly a help to the fire-raisers, unlike the threatening rain which would ruin their plan.

Heavy droplets bounced off the brim of his hat. Fawlkner despatched a silent prayer upstairs for the imminent downpour to be diverted elsewhere, anywhere but over Borrego. As if in answer to the entreaty, the impending rain ceased as quickly as it had started.

Fawlkner sighed with relief as he neared his first goal. His hands came together as he murmured a silent 'Thank you'.

He paused behind a deserted barn, then gingerly peered round the corner to ensure the coast was clear. Thankfully, there was nobody yet about. Catfooting across to the far corner of the theatre, he paused again, ears attuned to any suspicious sounds. A cat howled some distance away. Otherwise, only the soughing of the wind disturbed the silence propelling the storm clouds away to the north.

Unslinging his sack, Fawlkner quickly assembled the homemade fire-raising kit. The rags were doused in oil and pushed well underneath the floor of the building which, like all the others in the town, was erected above ground level on stilts with a gap of two feet.

Next came the ready-fused stick of dynamite positioned beside the rags which would substantially increase the rapid spread of the fire. The tiny stub of candle was set to ignite the fuse after approximately ten minutes.

A nervous look around, a struck vesta, and the candle was lit. Luckily there was no hint of a breeze at ground level. The candle sputtered, the wax slowly melting as the flame began its gradual descent. The rancher eyed the makeshift bomb. This would be his last chance to call off the drastic action. But already he knew that the moment for hesitation had passed.

Piecrust Pete would by now have set his own device on a collison course with destiny. The die had been well and truly cast.

Gathering up his equipment, Fawlkner cautiously crept along the back wall of the theatre. Stopping at an alleyway, he threw a wary look right towards the main street. All seemed clear.

He was about to cross to the far side when a man suddenly opened a door leading from the theatre and stepped out into the alley. It was the cleaner. The guy must have come in early to clear up from the previous night's entertainment. Fawlkner did not recognize him.

'Who in the name of Old Glory are you?' the guy demanded. He clearly did not recognize the local rancher. 'And what in tarnation are you creepin' around here for at this time in the mornin'?'

The truculent tone was as much a challenge as a surprised query. The rancher ignored the defiance and drew his pistol. But Stinkweed Randle was not to be intimidated. A lowly swamper he may be, but Jackson Drago had given him a job when others had shunned him. His loyalty to the theatre owner meant that he was no pushover.

Without any preamble Randle brought the broom he was holding down hard on to the outstretched gunhand. The pistol clattered to the floor. A growl of anger issued from the swamper's throat as he launched himself at this n'er-do-well snooper. The pair tumbled to the ground.

Over and over they rolled in the dust, each man trying to gain the upper hand. Punches were thrown, but none had the power for a knockout blow.

Initially taken by surprise, Fawlkner soon recovered. Although older, he was much bigger and stronger than the swamper and quickly gained the upper hand. Grappling for a superior hold, his hand brushed against the discarded revolver and grasped the butt firmly.

One almighty push and he managed to extricate himself from Randle's snake-like arms. The gun rose and came down with a dull thud on the guy's exposed head. It was sufficient to knock him out cold.

Fawlkner slithered from beneath the deadweight and lay on the ground panting from the unaccustomed exertion. His over-burdened heart pounded in his chest like an express locomotive. He wasn't used to such violent activity.

But this was no time for resting up. The candle was steadily burning down.

The unwelcome encounter with the swamper had cost valuable minutes. Nonetheless, the rancher's sense of justice meant he had to ensure the guy was not in any danger. Blood dribbing down a head wound did not bode well. The last thing he wanted was the responsibility of a dead man on his conscience.

Luckily, Stinkweed Randle was not badly hurt. Using the guy's own suspenders, he tied him up securely then moved him over behind a pile of logs some distance from the influence of the expected flames. A gag prevented any shouts for help when he regained consciousness.

It was with a profound sense of relief that the rancher ascertained that the confrontation had gone unnoticed. He quickly moved across the alley to repeated the incendiary procedure beneath the Palace.

In the meantime, Piecrust Pete had successfully laid his own bomb under the saddle shop. But it was while he was crawling beneath the emporium that he received a jolt to his part of the plan.

His acute hearing, already reconciled to any unusual noises, picked up the sound of squeaking and rustling.

Suddenly a pointed snout poked out of a hole. It was quickly followed by two more. Sharp teeth bared at this unwelcome intruder into their domain. Warriner's eyes popped.

Rats.

If there was one ceature on God's earth that Piecrust Pete detested, it was rats. Odious creatures with long tails and short hairy coats of grey fur, they invoke a spine-tingling dread in the old soldier. The sweat of terror bubbled up on his face. He would rather face a charging regiment of enemy soldiers any day than a nest of rats.

One of the rodents darted forward attempting to escape. Piecrust moved aside to avoid the loathsome rodent. Both collided.

The animal's automatic reaction was to snap out at this invader. Its pointed teeth bit deep into the man's cheek drawing blood. The victim could not suppress a cry of pain mingled with fear. He desperately scuttled backwards away from this repulsive threat, panic lending speed to his terror-stricken retreat.

The rat likewise fled the scene. But it was quickly replaced by four others. Back out in the alley, Piecrust breathed deep and hard struggling to control his racing heart. He gingerly peered under the building. Red eyes peered back.

Stalemate!

What could he do now? Abandoning the plan to blow up the emporium was tempting, but out of the question. Piecrust Pete Warriner might harbour secret fears, but he was no shirker. He knew where his duty lay. But time was passing quickly. The boss would have finished laying his bombs.

There was only one way to deal with the loathsome creatures.

Quickly he grabbed a handful of rags and doused them in oil. Girding up his nerve, the old soldier once again scrambled beneath the emporium. He was greeted by a line of bared teeth and high-pitched irate squealing that chilled his bones to the marrow.

A vesta was struck and applied to the rags which instantly flared up. The squealing intensified as the creatures backed away. Panic gripped the pack as the flaming terror drew closer. Then, as one they all disappeared back down into their hole. Warriner scuttled closer and thrust the burning heap into the mouth of the nest.

He lay on his back, mouth agape, praying that the nightmare was finally over. But there was no time for any further delay. With a renewed vigour, he prepared the final bomb making full use of the blazing rags. In a few minutes, those rats would be heading down into the Devil's fiery furnace.

In the meantime, Ben Fawlkner had already set the final charge beneath the Drago Palace. This one was to be the final and largest fire. And it would benefit from two sticks of dynamite as befitted its importance to the conniving kidnapper.

The laying of the charge proceeded as planned. Once completed, Fawlkner retraced his steps.

Arriving at the spot where they had left the horses and pack mule, the rancher settled down to await his sidekick.

Five minutes passed. He was getting worried. Where was Piecrust? Had something happened to him? Had he been spotted, just like he himself had almost been sussed? All manner of panic-laced question assailed his brain. It would not be long now before the first bomb exploded.

Again he looked at his watch.

The minutes were ticking inexorably by. Then he

saw him, scuttling crab-like up the slope, his boots slipping on the loose shale.

'I was getting worried about you,' Fawlkner averred with concern. 'Figured you'd been spotted.'

Sheer horror was etched across the old-timer's wizened features as he flopped down beside his boss.

'Gee, man!' exclaimed the rancher. 'You look like you've seen a ghost.'

'Worse than that,' gasped Warriner breathing hard.

Before he had time to account for his startling appearance, the first of the explosions rent the air. Both men turned as one towards the town. Nothing could be seen. It would take some minutes before the fire took hold. Seconds later the next building went up. The other two quickly followed.

Both men grinned at one another, vigorously shaking hands. Exultation overshadowed the grim consequences of what they had set in motion.

'We did it!' shouted a jubilant Pete Warriner, his spine-tingling incident with the rats forgotten.

ELEVEN

BEWARE OF GREEKS!

Much as they both appreciated that departing the scene ought to be a priority, the two old soldiers remained riveted to the spot. The low knoll on which they were secreted offered the perfect grandstand from which to view their handiwork. Smoke was now billowing forth, spiralling up into the early-morning sky like clutching tentacles.

Shouts of panic could be heard as Borrego was jerked awake to the grim reality that a conflagration had gripped the town. People could be seen running hither and thither. The two watchers gaped open-mouthed hypnotized by the rapidly escalating fire.

A bell began clanging. But this was no Sunday morning summons to church. The ringing tones assumed more of a warning. It was a summons for the town's fire crew to assemble and carry out the routine that all towns practised for just such an eventuality.

But they would have to be fast. Fires often spread rapidly, jumping from one wooden structure to another. Luckily for Borrego, the wind had dropped once the threatening storm had passed.

'Let's move across to that headland on the edge of town,' suggested Fawlkner. 'Then we can see when one of Drago's hired hands leaves to deliver the good news.'

Sliding down the backslope, they gathered up the horses and mule, walking them behind the cluster of trees so that nobody could observe their presence. Once ensconsed in their new position, all they could do was wait.

Sooner or later, somebody would have to inform the rancher that his properties had been consumed by fire. Not a task anybody would relish.

Now that he had time to contemplate the drastic action they had taken, Fawlkner silently urged the fire crews to get the blazes under control. He had no wish for the whole town to be consumed. All he wanted was for that skunk Jackson Drago to suffer for his ignominious abduction and threat to his daughter's life.

Certainly from what he could make out, the fires had indeed been contained within the precincts of the four buildings. He knew that all of them were empty at night.

Had there been people in residence, he would not have gone for the plan. No way did the rancher want anybody's untimely demise on his conscience.

His altercation with Stinkweed Randle was the only blot on an otherwise perfect job. The assault was bound to throw suspicion on the fact that the fires had been started deliberately. And the finger of accusation would most assuredly point his way once Drago was made of aware of the facts.

Ben Fawlkner was not bothered. By then, if everything went according to plan, his daughter would be free. And Jackson Drago would have to answer charges of abduction if he chose to make an issue of it.

In all the excitement, the rancher had clean forgotten the terror that had gripped his old sergeant when he had returned to their place of concealment. It was the sight of the bleeding tooth marks on his partner's face that prompted a reminder.

'You were about to tell me why you looked so terrified,' he posed, seeking enlightenment.

'Rats!' blurted out Piecrust shivering at the recall. 'There was a nest of the critters beneath the emporium. They must have been attracted by the sacks of grain in the store. I can't stand the little bastards. The sight of them varmints almost sent me over the edge, I can tell yuh.'

Fawlkner couldn't contain a gleeful chuckle.

'It's all right for you,' the old guy postulated, eliciting hurt pride. 'You didn't have to face 'em down like me.'

Piecrust went on to outline how he had managed to overcome his fear and carry on with the plan.

As they were musing on these matters, a rider burst through the pall of smoke. The guy was heading east in the direction of the Southern Cross. Fawlkner smiled with grim satisfaction. In a few hours, Drago would receive the news that his investments in Borrego had gone up in smoke.

He sure would be hopping mad. The rancher chuckled to himself. Now that was a sight he would like to have witnessed.

Giving the messenger ample time to eat dust, the two fire-raisers then headed back to the Big Dipper. All they could do now was trust that Del Gannon's part of the scheme would be as successful as their own.

Gannon had settled himself down for a long wait.

It would be some hours before the expected arrival of the harbinger of good tidings – bad if you were in Drago's boots. The lookout post he had selected was in some rocks as close to the Southern Cross as he could manage. Unfortunately, it was still a half-mile away from the cluster of buildings where he could only assume Daisy was being held captive.

Drago had chosen the site for his headquarters well: no chance of being caught unawares by a surprise attack. Flat ground enclosed the ranch with barely a spike of grass between it and the nearest cover where Del was located. Fawlkner had made a particular issue of this problem.

And it was Piecrust Pete who had come up with a solution.

It involved a Californian variation on the ancient Greek legend of the Trojan Horse. In this case, making use of the flat-bed wagon.

A powerful telescope had been deemed necessary for picking out details of the ranch and its occupants. The scope was of solid ex-army issue. Old Piecrust Warriner had come to the rescue once again. That guy had more aces up his sleeve than a professional cardsharp.

Towards the latter end of the war he had been a sniper assigned to Ulysses Grant for the Union general's protection. The 'scope had been given to him as a personal memento by the man himself.

Pin-pointing various people and what they were up to helped pass the time while Del waited. So far there had been no sighting of the girl. Her abductors were clearly keeping their ace of hearts under close guard inside the main house.

It was towards noon when a cloud of yellow dust caught the watcher's attention. The 'scope picked out a single rider going hell-for-leather. A prim smile crossed the tanned visage. The guy's hurried arrival appeared to confirm that Ben Fawlkner and Piecrust had been successful in their fire-raising endeavour.

The newcomer skidded to a halt outside the ranch house and hurried inside. Five minutes passed before a big man appeared. It was Drago. He was fastening on his gunbelt. Arms waving frantically like a demented windmill, he issued orders which saw a half-dozen hands scurrying off in the direction of the corral to saddle up.

Del was keeping his fingers crossed that the ranch boss would be so concerned for his Borrego holdings that no thought would have been given to the notion that this could be a set-up to lure him away from the ranch. Panic is apt to blur a man's thinking.

And so it proved in this case.

The three men who were being left behind to guard the girl stood on the veranda watching their buddies ride away.

Del's fist screwed up into a tight ball when he recognized one of them as being the pesky galoot who had bushwhacked him and stolen his rifle. Cabel Sharkey slouched against the veranda support acting as if he owned the place. Del's prized Winchester was resting in the crook of his arm.

Although at the moment, retrieval of the *One in a Thousand* was of secondary importance to freeing the girl.

The Southern Cross riders galloped away led by Jackson Drago. Passing below where the watcher was hidden, they disappeared in the direction of Borrego. The three men left behind went back into the house. Del was not worried for the safety of their captive. It was in all their interests to ensure she remained unharmed.

That proviso naturally applied only until the bill of sale transferring ownership of Big Dipper property into Drago's hands had been handed over. If everything went according to plan, it never would be.

Five minutes passed, during which time Del scanned the outbuildings for any signs of movement. The telescope panned across the corral, the blacksmith's shop, barn, haystore, toolshed and bunkhouse. Nothing.

The time had arrived to make his move.

A momentary hesitation dogged his limbs, not fear for himself – just a realization that the next hour could be placing Daisy's life in danger. Lead was going to fly, and once that happened, there was no telling who would be on the receiving end.

A tiny wren perched on the rock near his head. The jaunty warble appeared to be urging its new buddy into motion.

'You're right, little fella,' murmured Del scrambling down the back slope to where he had left the wagon. 'This ain't no time for getting cold feet.' The bird twittered its agreement then flew off.

Secured to the bench seat of the wagon was the replica of a man made from old clothes and stuffed with straw. A hat had been fastened to its head. Near to, there was no mistaking it as a dummy. But from a distance, it gave the appearance of a real human being.

'This is where you do your stuff, mister,' said Del, climbing into the bed of the wagon and concealing himself.

Before moving off, he checked his revolver together with a spare carbine. Satisfied, he slapped the feathers lightly across the horse's rump. The animal moved forward at a steady jog.

Once out in the open, the wagon was in clear view from the ranch.

Sharkey slammed the door of the back bedroom where he had been checking the bonds of the ransomed prize.

With his boss suddenly heading for Borrego at a fast clip, an idea had impinged itself on the devious mind of his new gunhand. With only three men left to look after the girl, questions as to how he could turn this new development to his own advantage found Cabel Sharkey thinking hard.

Getting his hands on the black stones would be too involved. He had no idea where they were to be found. The discovery had occurred before he joined the Drago payroll. What he needed was a get-rich-quick scheme with little chance of failure.

A straight exchange was the best option – the girl for a suitable ransom, say five thousand bucks. After all, he didn't want to be greedy. And he was sure that Fawlkner could raise that amount with no difficulty by remortgaging his ranch.

He threw a knowing look towards the room he had only just vacated. Due to her incessent tirade of empty threats as to what would befall the abductor if she were not released, Drago had personally gagged her.

The girl sure was a looker. Before he made the exchange, Sharkey intended to have some fun with her. And he intended to make certain she was a sight more co-operative as well.

A serious mien replaced the lascivious gleam of moments before. But if his scheme were to have any chance of succeeding, he would have to act straight away. Drago would not be back for some time and Sharkey would need to be far away by then.

A tight-lipped resolve soured the hardcase's face. First off though, he would need to rub out those other two knuckleheads who had also been left behind. No problem for a gunslinger of Sharkey's calibre.

Before he had time to work out how best to get rid of them, a shout came from down below.

'Hey, Sharkey! Get down here, pronto!'

Hammerfall Johansen was a highly skilled blacksmith and farrier. The burly Swede resented this newcomer being left in charge while the boss was away. The snarled tone held no respect for the gunman's elevated position.

Sharkey gritted his teeth. Nobody spoke to him like that. He would definitely enjoy snuffing out that pesky foreigner.

'What is it?' he rapped back without moving.

'We got visitor,' came the puzzled response. 'I not recognize him.'

Sharkey moved across to the window at the end of the upstairs corridor. He peered out, his thick eyebrows meeting in the middle as he frowned. Who in tarnation was this? He sure didn't need any visitors wasting his time.

'Have Ventana go to see what he wants, then get rid of him,' he shouted back. 'The last thing we need is some nosey neighbour calling for a palaver.'

Hunkered down behind the mannequin, Del narrowed his gaze. Steadily, the main ranch building loomed closer. A hundred yards out, a blunt shout to haul up was issued from a ranch hand who had appeared on the veranda.

The order was ignored, the wagon continuing on its direct course to the outer gate that had been left ajar when Drago and his boys departed.

Again the summons came, this time with a threatening intent. 'Haul up, *hombre*,' came the terse order accompanied by the levering of a round into the Spencer rifle, 'or taste lead. This ees your last chance.' A hint of panic gripped the Mexican speaker's lyrical cadence.

Still no response from the wagon driver.

Del held his breath. Not much further to go before the supposed wagon driver was sussed. But the closer he could get to the ranch without the dummy being spotted, the easier it would be to take out the hoodwinked adversary.

A loud blast from the Spencer broke the deadlock. Instantly the head of the dummy cowpoke erupted in a shower of straw. So stunned was the cowboy that he just stood there, riveted to the spot.

'Drop the rifle!'

Del's strident command jerked the greaser out of his stupor. The guy ignored the command bringing the rifle unto his shoulder. But Del was ready. His own rifle barked. A bullet struck the cowpoke in the chest, dead centre, dead being the operative word. Ventana crumpled to the floor.

One down, two to go.

The wagon drew closer to the ranch.

With the Mexican lying in the dust, the front downstairs window was knocked out. A hand appeared holding a gun and hot lead began peppering the wagon. Lances of orange flame spat forth. Del was forced to hug the flatbed behind the dummy as slivers of wood flew off in all directions.

The attacker was faced with a serious dilemma. His Trojan Horse plan to close with the ranch had worked perfectly. But now he had run slap bang into a brick wall. How in thunder was he going to get past the hidden defenders to rescue the girl? He hadn't given that aspect enough consideration.

All he could do for the moment was return fire and pray that he hit another of the kidnappers before they got him. The odds in favour of him succeeding were not great. A radical solution was needed.

After five minutes of heavy gunfire, there was a sudden lull. Was the guy reloading? Maybe this would be his chance. While he was considering this scenario, more firing opened up. It originated from a window on the upper floor. But there were only three shots fired before they ceased as well.

A tense silence settled over the battle zone.

Del knew that he could not wait around indefinitely. He had to do something. And that meant moving from his current exposed position. Slapping the leathers, he manoeuvred the wagon over to the barn. No further shots pursued him. That in itself seemed very strange. Had the defenders anticipated his change of plan and were already waiting in ambush?

Urging the horse-drawn wagon behind the barn, he rolled off and scuttled behind a water trough. Still no response. Cat-like and stealthy, he crept along the side of the barn and peered round the corner. The only thing that disturbed the stillness was the ranch cat clutching a mouse between its teeth. The animal seemed oblivious to the deathly interaction being played out.

Del sucked in a deep breath and launched himself across the open gap separating the barn from the ranch house. Bent low, he ran towards the front door. There he stood for a moment flat against the outer wall listening. No sound reached his straining ears. So he leaned across and released the door catch nudging it open.

Flinging himself into the entrance hall, he rolled once coming to his feet, sixgun panning the room. Then he saw him. A man lay unmoving below the broken window. He was clearly dead judging by the amount of blood staining the carpet around the still body.

Del quickly dodged behind a large suit of armour. From that strange place of concealment, he kept a wary eye on the staircase from where he expected the other gunman to make his lethal presence felt. But nobody appeared. Seconds passed, seeming like hours. Nothing. Not a murmur disturbed the macabre scene.

Charily, Del stood up and approached the body of Hammerfall Johansen. And that is when he received a brutal shock. The stunning jolt was barely creditable. But it was true.

The blacksmith had been shot in the back.

That discovery could mean only one thing. The third man had his own agenda regarding the disposal of their captive. Del sensed the perpetration of a double-cross by Cabel Sharkey.

Without further ado, he dashed up the stairs. There was nobody to be seen. And at the end of the corridor, a rear door stood open. Swinging slowly in the gentle breeze, its squeaking hinges answered Del's silent question. Desperation for the girl's safety sent him scurrying through the hushed rooms praying that he would find her. But to no avail.

The house was empty.

At the end of the corridor, he looked out of the front window. The pastoral scene was marred by the dead body of the Mexican cowboy. But that was not his concern. What concerned him more was the fact that Daisy Fawlkner had been abducted yet again.

Then something happened to raise Del's hopes.

TWELVE

A BOLT FROM THE BLUE

Over on the far side of the corral, a man had emerged from the tool shed. He peered gingerly around as if to confirm that the recent shoot-out was over. A closer look revealed him to be no more than a youngster, and a Mexican judging by the tattered sombero and white cotton suit worn by *peons.*

Del took the stairs three at a time, hurrying outside.

'Howdie there, muchacho,' he called across, injecting a light-hearted bounce into the greeting so as not to frighten the kid off. The boy turned to run away. 'I mean you no harm,' Del persisted, holding his hands skyward away from his holstered gun. 'All I am after is some information.'

The boy hesitated, then came forward slowly.

'My name is Delaware Gannon,' the white man declared holding out his hand in a friendly gesture. 'A lady has been held captive here and I have come to set her free. Do you know where she is now?'

The boy was about fourteen years of age and it transpired after some gentle prompting that his name was Juan Carlos and he was employed by Drago as a general labourer around the ranch. His father was a business colleague of the rancher. Drago had agreed to take the boy on as an apprentice under the guidance of the blacksmith, Hammerfall Johansen. Both being of foreign descent, the pair had gelled like moss to a rock.

Tears welled in the boy's eyes when Del relayed the sad tidings that his mentor had been killed, shot in the back.

'That was bad man boss took on for hired gun.' The raging invective was interspersed with Spanish expletives. 'I hate heem.'

'You talking about Cabel Sharkey, boy?' rapped Del.

A brisk nod of accord was accompanied by an angry lob of spittle into the dust at the mention of the vile name.

'Then maybe you and me can help each other out.'

Del's eyes gleamed with hope. Suddenly, from being consumed by abject despair, a wave of expectation had been resurrected. 'Did you see which direction he took with the lady?'

Without hesitation, Juan Carlos pointed towards the east.

Del ruffled the boy's thick matt of black hair. 'Much obliged, *amigo*,' he declared avidly. 'I won't forget your help when I catch up with that *villano*.'

The boy pointed his finger and shouted, 'Bang! Bang!'

'Only if'n he chooses to play it that way.' said Del knowing the varmint held a distinct advantage with the special rifle. 'The main thing is to rescue the lady.' Now that he knew the trail that Sharkey had taken, Del was anxious to get after him. 'You gotten a horse I could borrow?' he asked.

Juan Carlos hustled away returning some minutes later with a roan which was saddled and ready.

Mounting up, Del wished the Mexican boy a brisk *adios* and spurred off towards the distant Vallecito Mountains.

So eager was Sharkey to escape from the Southern Cross with his hostage that he had paid little heed to the clear trail he was leaving. A pursuer of Del Gannon's worth had no difficulty dogging the two sets of tracks. By early afternoon, he had come across the ashes of a fire. Close by was a dark stain in the sand where the dregs from a coffee pot had been emptied.

It had to be Sharkey and the girl.

He despatched a fervent prayer upstairs that she had been left unharmed. He knew that Daisy would not have gone willingly. He also knew that Cabel Sharkey would not balk at delivering his own brand of heavy-handed justice to quash her feisty disposition.

Feeling the blackened remains of the fire he was able to estimate that his quarry was no more than an hour ahead.

Remounting, he spurred away. His meal of a stick of jerky and some dried biscuits washed down with tepid water was taken in the saddle.

According to the angle of the sun, they appeared to be slanting to the right making in a broad half-circle. Such a course would bring them on to the edge of Big Dipper land. Del's conjecture that Sharkey intended double-crossing his employer appeared to be holding water. The route would also take them somewhere close to where he and Daisy had initially discovered the black gold.

Del wondered if the gunslinger had any notion of the potential fortune over which he was riding. If he had, maybe he would regard the presence of the girl as a hindrance rather than an asset. The thought brought sweat bubbling out on his brow.

He urged the roan to a steady gallop, anxious to run his quarry to ground.

Some three miles ahead, Sharkey had become tired of the girl's carping. He had reapplied the gag to shut her up. His intention was to hide the girl in a cave he had discovered while negotiating the switch with Fawlkner, then wait there while the rancher secured the dough. In so doing, he would not get any trouble from Drago. That was the plan.

But first he had another problem to solve.

Although a ruthless and predatory killer, Cabel Sharkey was a shrewd gambler. Over the last hour, the gunslick had become aware that his trail was being followed. The pursuer had not given himself away. But Sharkey possessed that vital sixth sense that had enabled him to avoid the long arm of the law for so long.

Frequent halts to observe their backtrail by her abductor were enough to make Daisy likewise aware that somebody was following. Hope of an imminent rescue registered in her flickering gaze.

This posed no worries for the kidnapper. Indeed he welcomed the chance to rid himself of this niggling encumbrance. After all, didn't he have the Special rifle and plenty of time to lay an ambush?

And he intended to make full use of it.

Rounding a bend in the trail, he saw a small copse of trees which was ideal for his plan. Veering behind it, he tied off the horses making certain they were out of sight. Displaying no concern for the girl's comfort, he dragged her out of the saddle and securely pinioned her to a tree.

'This is where your knight in shining armour meets a better adversary,' rasped the killer, jacking a round into the Winchester. Daisy struggled against her bonds, but to no avail. Sharkey grinned down at her. A calloused hand pawed at her dirt-smeared cheek. 'You and me is gonna have some fun once this pesky boil has been lanced.'

The girl shivered, attempting unsuccessfully to draw away. The enraged look in her eyes made Sharkey all the more excited.

'That's it, gal,' he exhorted her. 'You show me

some spirit. I like a gal that ain't meek and mild.' Then his face assumed the twisted snarl of a rabid dog. 'But first . . . the boil.'

He moved across to a cluster of rocks and climbed up to the top to await the approach of his victim.

It was another half-hour before the steady clippety clop of a cantering horse reached his ears.

Sharkey's body stiffened.

The guy trotted round the bend completely oblivious to his impending fate. Sharkey was surprised to see that his pursuer was none other than Del Gannon. He almost laughed out loud. This was better than he could ever have wished for. Rubbing out this turkey was an added bonus and no mistake.

He allowed the rider to pass unmolested. Only when he had passed the copse did the killer open fire. The deep-throated roar from the Special cut the air like a knife through butter. The rider clutched at his head before toppling from the saddle.

An evil smile cracked the killer's granite features. A perfect shot.

Quickly he scrambled down from his perch and approached the still form. The rifle barrel poked at the body.

'On your feet, dog breath,' growled the bushwhacker. 'I know you ain't dead. Killing you is gonna be face to face so's you can see it coming.'

Del groaned. The bullet had seared his skull. A bloody line had ripped away his left ear lobe momentarily stunning him.

'Now weren't that the finest piece of shooting you

ever did see?' warbled Sharkey stepping back to cover his victim. 'They sure weren't kidding about this rifle being special.'

'Where's the girl?' The query emerged as a croaking rasp. Del's first thought had been for Daisy's safety.

'Don't you fret none about her,' replied Sharkey. 'She's OK. A bit mussed up, but in one piece. And I fully intend to get a good price for her as well when her father coughs up to get his precious daughter back.'

'So I was right,' Del muttered under his breath.

'Enough talk,' rapped the killer bringing the rifle up to his shoulder. 'This palaver is costing me time. Say your prayers, sucker.'

The killer's finger tightened on the trigger. Del's eyed bulged as he saw the grim reaper staring at him down the end of the gun barrel.

But the expected blast of hot lead never came.

Sharkey's back arched, his mouth gaping wide, eyes staring in total confusion. The rifle dropped from his hands as he stumbled forward, crashing on to his face. Del was also left stupefied.

For stuck in the killer's back was an arrow.

A lone figure stepped out from behind a clump of desert willow. Nearby a chuckawalla scampered out of his way as Lone Wolf ambled across the stony terrain. The supremely accurate shot must have been all of seventy-five yards.

Del tried to focus on his saviour, but blood from the wound and a stabbing headache threatened to overwhelm him. The young brave ran up and grabbed him before he fell.

'Where'd you spring from, buddy?' Del gasped out. 'Figured I was a goner for sure.'

Then he realized that the boy could not understand his tongue. A few choice signs and Lone Wolf was able to relate that he had been despatched by the tribal elders to seek out more of the mysterious black stones.

'It's lucky for me that you came along at the right moment,' Del gestured. But the pain from his injury prevented any further communication. His final sign was for the boy to locate the girl and release her.

Lone Wolf laid his friend down against a rock and went in search of Daisy. The pair soon returned and Del's wound was expertly attended to. He was relieved to hear that she had suffered no real ill-treatment at the hands of the kidnappers. Although Sharkey's carnal intentions had Lone Wolf not come on the scene didn't bear thinking about.

'Seems like you fixing me up is becoming a habit,' muttered Del through a blurred haze. But the pain inside his head was still throbbing madly.

The Indian frowned, then returned to his horse. Unhitching a buckskin supply pack he delved inside. Del was then told to chew on the dark root which would alleviate the pain. And sure enough, ten minutes later, the rampant bull stomping around inside his head had completely disappeared.

Natural remedies from the land are always the best was Lone Wolf's silent assertion. Del wasn't about to argue the point.

He then introduced the Indian to Daisy.

'This is the Yuma brave that I told you about,' he said.

'Would you ask him to accompany us back to the ranch?' the girl submitted. 'There might be more of Drago's men around. And those shots would lead them right here.'

Lone Wolf was more than happy to accede to her proposal.

A half-hour later, Del was ready to ride. But first he wandered over to the dead outlaw and secured the prize rifle that was his of right.

'Might as well see what this ugly galoot is packing,' he muttered to himself rifling through the dead killer's pockets. 'Maybe he has a price on his head.'

And that was when another shock struck with the force of a loco mule.

'Something wrong, Del?' asked Daisy anxiously noting the bewildered expression clouding the Texan's face. Walking over she saw what he now had resting in the palm of an outstretched hand.

It was as if he had not heard the question. He just stood there, staring at the object in his hand.

A pocket watch, but no ordinary timepiece: this one had belonged to his partner. It was a family heirloom that Johnny Concho's father had passed down to his son.

He flipped open the lid releasing a haunting melody that drifted on the static air. A glassy faraway look transfixed the ex-bronc rider. The sombre tune's mellifluous air held him in a mesmeric grip. It was in stark contrast to the killing ground upon which the three comrades now stood. Finally it stumbled to a close.

The girl placed a hand on his arm.

The intimate gesture brought Del out of his trance.

He snapped the watch shut before explaining its significance.

'This watch belonged to my partner before this piece of scum stabbed him to death in a Yuma alleyway.' A reptilian sneer precipitated a brutal kick to the dead man's corpse. 'I never knew until this moment that it was Cabel Sharkey who killed the poor kid. It's just a shame that Lone Wolf got in first preventing me from personally sending the bloodsucker downstairs.'

'Be glad that he did,' Daisy reminded the distraught man. 'Otherwise it would have been you lying there now and not him.'

Even through the pain of reliving the grizzly truth about Johnny's demise, Del recognized that the girl was right. He owed his life to the Yuma brave. Now he could bury the vengeful hurt that had been eating away at his soul since that melancholy day.

'You're right, Daisy,' he said carefully, slipping the watch into his own pocket. 'Now I can look to the future.'

Del made a promise to himself that someday, he would return the piece to someone who deserved it far more than some thieving outlaw.

That was when another thought struck him. The stolen money! Hurriedly, he delved into the killer's saddle-bags. And there it was, tied up securely in the same hessian sack. Some of it was missing but the bulk was intact. He secured the heavy bag to his own saddle before mounting up. Perhaps that orange farm was now within his grasp after all.

However, there was still the matter of Jackson Drago and his chicanery to be dealt with. On the way back to the ranch he filled Daisy in on his dream.

THIRTEEN

NO PLACE FOR QUITTERS

By the time the owner of the Southern Cross reached Borrego, the fires had been doused. Luckily no other properties were damaged. Only Drago's holdings had suffered. Indeed, there was virtually nothing left to salvage. For five minutes the rancher just sat on his horse staring at the smouldering remains of his burgeoning empire. All his plans had gone up in smoke.

Dismounting, he trudged among the charred ruins, muttering low imprecations to himself. Gradually, distress turned to anger. Somebody was going to pay dearly for this outrage. He already harboured a growing suspicion as to who was behind the blatant challenge.

It was when he returned to the street that he felt somebody tugging at his arm. Turning slowly, eyes like chips of flint focused on to the manager of the Drago Palace.

Normally attired in the manner of a sartorially urbane overseer, Ezra Janks was bedraggled and dirty. His pristine white shirt was torn and smoke-stained. Behind him stood Stinkweed Randle.

'Was anything left of the Palace?' Drago rasped.

Janks swallowed nervously. ' 'Fraid not, Mr Drago,' he burbled, wringing his pudgy hands. 'But the cleaner here' – he pushed Stinkweed to the fore, anxious that any repercussions should not fall on his shoulders – 'disturbed the guy who started the fires.'

The cleaner quickly butted in. 'I tried to stop him, boss, but the fella slugged me. Took me by surprise he did. Near on caved in my skull.' Randle rubbed the large lump protruding from his head.

Drago impatiently waved aside the swamper's woes.

'Did you recognize him?' he snapped.

'He sure was a big fella. An oldish dude with grey hair I could see it was grey under that Union hat he was wearing.'

'Was it an officer's hat?' Drago shot back.

Randle nodded. 'Reckon it was at that.'

An ugly snarl issued from between clenched teeth. He slammed a bunched fist into the palm of his hand.

There was only one man around these parts who wore such a hat. Without further preamble, he issued orders for all the goods that could be salvaged to be placed in a wagon and transported back to the

Southern Cross in due course.

'What do we do now, boss?' enquired his foreman, Isaac Hayes.

'We head back to the ranch and make sure that' – Drago paused not wanting any onlookers to suspect his other scheme which could now be under threat – 'our guest is still enjoying her visit to the Southern Cross.'

There was nothing more he could do here. The main thing now was to prevent Fawlkner getting his daughter back. He cursed himself for having fallen for what seemed such an obvious trick. He had badly underestimated the resourcefulness of his adversary.

But when it came down to it, didn't Jackson Drago hold all the aces? He had more men, including the hired gunman who was guarding the girl. How could one old rancher well past his prime helped by a crazy old-timer possibly think to outwit the might of the Southern Cross?

With that thought in mind, the martinet felt his spirits lifting. There was no way that his plan to take over the whole Anza Valley was going to be thwarted. The black gold would be his, and the Borrego holdings rebuilt.

A dreamy cast suffused the blackguard's rubicund features as he dragged on the reins, leading the way back to the ranch. Maybe he would even rename the town Dragoville.

Even before the band of riders came in sight of the Southern Cross ranch, Drago sensed that something was wrong. It was that same feeling he had during the war when the blue bellies had been lying in ambush.

He slowed to a steady canter. Jogging across the open sward surrounding the ranch buildings, nothing seemed out of place. Nothing moved. And that was the problem. Three men had been left behind plus the Mexican kid. Surely somebody would have emerged to greet them.

Then he saw what looked like a bundle of discarded laundry in front of the main house. Drawing closer, a sharp intake of breath from Hayes brought the riders to an abrupt halt.

'Ain't that Ventana?' posed one nervous cowboy staring at the bloody corpse.

'Looks like he's dead.' The comment from another needed no clarification. The Mexican would not be propositioning the Borrego *señoritas* anymore.

But what of the others? Drago was thinking especially about the girl.

The men shuffled edgily, restive hands toying with gun butts. An aura of menace hung over the ranch gripping their vitals.

The ranch boss shook off the uneasy paralysis that was threatening to overwhelm him. Dismounting he drew his pistol and stepped up on to the veranda. The front door hung ajar, one more clue pointing to dark deeds having been performed during his absence.

And inside the entrance hall lay the dead body of Hammerfall Johansen.

Hayes pointed his gun at the Swede's body. 'Look! He's been shot in the back.' Nervous eyes panned the hall. 'And where's that new gunslinger?'

Drago had posed the same question to himself.

'Search the place from top to bottom,' he ordered his men curtly. He was already dashing up the stairs to the room where he had left the girl.

As he had expected, the room was devoid of its unwilling occupant. Everything indicated that Daisy Fawlkner had been whisked away. It seemed inconceivable that her father along with that lunkhead Warriner could have overcome a hard-bitten gunman and two other tough *hombres* as well.

Drago paced the room trying to figure out the cause of the mysterious disappearance. His disquieted cogitating was interrupted by a harsh shout from outside.

'Down here, boss!'

For a man of his bulk, Drago was no slouch when speed was of the essence. He descended the ornate staircase like a young colt.

Two hands were dragging a reluctant Juan Carlos across the corral. The *peon* had been discovered in the tool shack. He had not shifted since the kind *bondadoso gringo* had left some hours previously. The grim look on his patron's face made him wish that he had left with the *gringo.*

The cowboys threw him down on to the ground at Drago's feet. The boss had forgotten all about the kid. Now he stood over the trembling *peon,* legs apart, hands resting on his broad hips.

'You got some'n to tell me, Juan?' he hissed, skewering the boy to the ground with a baleful glare.

'I know nothing, *señor,*' he blurted out desperately attempting to scrabble away. 'Man come. When shooting start, Juan Carlos keep head down. Hide in tool shack. I see nothing.'

Without uttering another word, Drago held out his hand. A large bullwhip filled the giant paw. He shook out the deadly scourge. The brown rawhide coiled and twisted like an angry serpent. A quick flick brought forth a sharp crack that sliced open the fetid air.

'Let's see if'n my friend here can persuade your memory to return.' The reptilian grin held no trace of humour. 'Tie him to that wagon wheel, boys.'

Isaac Hayes frowned. He did not like the way things were shaping up. Indeed, he was unhappy with this whole damn business. Sure, he had gone along with Drago's attempts to get control of the Big Dipper. Even kidnapping the girl had been reluctantly overlooked. And look what had happened? Men had been shot dead and the whole thing was threatening to blow up into a range war.

If Fawlkner was willing to bite back, the other small operators in the valley would likely follow suit. This did not look good.

He had been with Drago from the beginning. But the guy was becoming unhinged, so fanatical had become his obsession with the black stones. That's what the acquisition of gold did to a man, drove him to the brink of madness and beyond. He stepped forward, grasping the whip-hand before it could deliver the first stroke.

'This ain't no way to act, boss,' he declared. 'Let me handle the kid. I'll soon get him to open up.'

But Drago's blood was up. He shook off the foreman's grip and knocked him to the ground.

'How dare you show me up in front of the boys,' he railed, swinging the whip and bringing it down hard across Hayes' shoulders. 'This is my ranch. I'm the law around here. So while you're working for me, you'll do as I say.' His face was bloated, purple with anger.

'Then I quit!'

Hayes scrambled away from the biting flick of the whip. He'd had enough.

'I ain't working for a mad man,' the ex-foreman's voice convulsed. Shock at being brutally assaulted by the man he had once considered a friend was mingled with sadness that things had come to this. 'You've changed, Jackson. And it sure ain't for the better.'

Hayes turned his back on the inflamed rancher and walked over to his horse.

'Stop right where you are,' snarled Drago. 'Nobody quits the Southern Cross unless I say so.'

Ignoring the blunt order, he swung into the saddle. The other hands remained silent, unmoving, mesmerized by the unexpected showdown. Hayes nudged the horse towards the open gate of the corral. His back, upright and rigid like a rocky pinnacle, held no fear of his old sidekick.

'One last chance, Hayes,' called Drago. There was still no reaction from the ageing cowboy who continued on his way.

Throwing down the whip, Drago moved across to his horse and withdrew his rifle. Jacking a round up the spout, he aimed it at the departing rider's back. Teeth gritted, lips drawn back in a deathly rictus, he pulled the trigger. A single tongue of flame burst forth.

The shot was dead centre, a splash of red erupting from the rider's back. Hayes threw up his arms and tumbled into the dust.

Barely catching his breath, Drago turned and pointed the gun at the Mexican boy. 'Now talk, greaser, or get a dose of the same medicine.'

Juan Carlos had seen enough. He tripped over his tongue desperately trying to babble out all that had happened since the mysterious gunfighter had attacked the ranch earlier that day.

'You did well to see sense, Juan,' Drago gently chided the boy. 'Although it's a shame I had to kill a man just to make you open up.' The rifle rose again. 'A crying shame to be sure.'

Another shot rang out. And another traitor bit the dust.

Drago then spun on his heel to face the group of stunned cowhands. The gun panned across them before the rancher placed it back in its scabbard.

'You boys help me to get rid of that skunk Fawlkner once and for all' – he paused, eyeing them with a caustic gaze before continuing – 'and I'll pay you each a hundred-dollar bonus. And when we've rubbed out Fawlkner we'll go after Sharkey and the girl.' He smiled at them but the drawn-back lips resembled a hungry alligator. 'Anybody who wants to quit can draw his pay and just ride off with no hard feelings.'

Nobody moved. Wary glances passed between the men. Scuffed boots nervously toed the sand. They had seen what happened to guys who tried pulling out. The evidence was written in blood before their eyes. Nobody quit the employ of Jackson Drago before he was good and ready.

'So are you in, boys?' breezed the chirpy rancher.

Tentative nods all round.

'Glad to hear it,' he said with a distinct edge to the remark. 'You made a wise choice. Now clear up this mess and be ready to ride at first light.'

FOURTEEN

SHOWDOWN

Coming in sight of the Big Dipper ranch house, Del signalled his comrades to haul rein on the crest of a low rise overlooking the settlement. Searching eyes probed every nook and cranny for evidence that other less friendly visitors were in the vicinity.

'See anything?' he asked, aiming the question specifically at Lone Wolf. He knew that Indians were much more aware of their surroundings than white folks.

The Yuma brave's eagle gaze scanned the raw terrain. A brief shake of the head elicited a nod of satisfaction from the Texan.

A twist of smoke rose into the air from the stone chimney indicating the house was occupied, although there was no sign of the residents.

Del voiced the conclusion they had all reached. 'Looks like your pa played his part and got back safely.'

'I'd be a sight happier if'n they'd show themselves,' she replied warily.

'Yeah,' Del agreed.

For a minute they sat looking down on the tranquil setting. It was Lone Wolf who made the suggestion that he should venture down the slope to ascertain that all was indeed as peaceful as it appeared.

Weaving between the loose stands of pine, he made a wide circle around the property without revealing himself. At the far side, he signalled that all was well. Del led the way down the slope. When they emerged into the open, the door of the ranch opened and Ben Fawlkner appeared.

Following a momentary hesitation before recognition registered, he then hurried across to greet the welcome arrivals. The girl threw herself off the horse and into her father's outstretched arms.

All the tension of the previous twelve hours came flooding out. Tears flowed like rain water off a roof as the pair embraced. The repulsion and fear of being abducted was overshadowed by the dread of not knowing if she would ever see her loved ones again.

Finally they parted.

'Well we did it,' gasped the rancher hugging the girl close. Relief at having his daughter safely back was starkly etched across the beaming visage.

'And that hired gunslinger won't be troubling us no more,' said Del. 'Although it would have been a different matter if'n Lone Wolf here hadn't turned up when he did.'

He indicated the Indian sitting astride his grey apaloosa pony like a rock sentinel. Only then did Fawlkner notice the youth.

'He don't speak our tongue,' Del informed the rancher, 'so we have to communicate through sign language.'

'Then you tell this fella how grateful I am for his help in getting my daughter back,' gushed Fawlkner gesturing for the Indian to dismount and come forward. 'And anything that I can do for him that's within my power is his for the asking.'

Del didn't need to translate the offer. He knew exactly what Lone Wolf would have said. That was the reason he was in this neck of the woods. The fact that a Yuma Indian was this far from his natural homeland had not occurred to the rancher. So intense had been his relief at having his daughter back in the fold that all other considerations had been eclipsed.

This omission was remedied by Del's promulgation that the boy had come to California to procure some more of the black stones.

'The Yuma look on them as good luck charms,' he asserted. 'And it's sure worked for us, him turning up at just the right moment.'

'Well, you tell this young fella that as far as I'm concerned, he can have all he wants.' He stroked the head of his faithful wolfhound. 'And if'n Drago wants them as well, I'll be willing to offer him a fair share to leave us alone.'

This pronouncement was met with surprise, and a sceptical glower from Piecrust. 'Let's hope that the varmint is just as accommodating as you, boss.' The old-timer's moustache twitched. 'But I ain't gonna hold my breath. Now how's about we eat afore the grub gets cold.'

They all trooped into the house and sat down at the table. All except Lone Wolf who chose to eat cross-legged on the floor. Piecrust was pleased, however, to note that he nonetheless lived up to his name by wolfing down the vittles in double quick time.

'Another helping?' There was no need for that enquiry to be translated. The cook beamed. 'This kid sure appreciates good grub when he tastes it.'

Whistling a tuneless melody, he then went outside to fill the water bucket.

'Do you really think that devious critter will give up on his obsession to grab the Big Dipper?' asked Del tearing off a lump of fresh baked bread and wiping off his plate with relish. 'The guy's scheme has been turned on its head. And he sure ain't gonna be one happy dude when he finds out we've gotten Daisy out of his clutches.'

Fawlkner considered his answer carefully before replying. 'I'd be willing to let bygones be bygones if'n he's willing to let us live here in peace. That heap of gold ain't worth all the trouble it's caused.' He looked across at the guzzling Indian. 'It may bring his tribe luck, but all it's brought us is a basketful of heartaches.'

A thoughtful silence descended over the small gathering.

Del speared a succulent chunk of beef on his plate. The fork lifted – but never reached his open mouth.

Outside a volley of rifle fire blasted apart the peaceful ambience within the cabin. An acute howl of pain cut through the sudden and unexpected shock that they were under attack. And that cry could only have come from Piecrust Warriner. In a second, Fawlkner was on his feet. He lunged for the door and dragged it open.

The old soldier lay splayed out in the dust, his body riddled with half-a-dozen bullet holes. He would not be making any more of his renowned apple pies. Framed in the doorway, the distraught rancher offered a sitting target for the bushwackers. More bullets peppered the doorpost inches from his head.

Del hauled the stricken man back inside the cabin and slammed the door.

A large sliver of wood had skewered his cheek. Blood was pouring from the ugly wound. Daisy wasted no time in sitting him down on the floor and attending to the injury. Meanwhile, a steady stream of gunfire began rattling the log house. The recently repaired front window was once again blown apart, glass flying everywhere.

The assault continued for five minutes before stumbling to an eerie halt.

The fearsome cacophany of moments before was replaced by a deathly voice easily recognized as that belonging to Jackson Drago.

'You got one last chance to sign over your holding, Fawlkner,' came the blunt threat. 'Otherwise it ends here.' A macabre laugh sent a chilled ripple slithering down Daisy's spine. 'For you that is. I ain't leaving and you ain't going nowhere. My boys have got you covered. Come out with your hands held high and I'll be generous and let you go free.'

But the defenders knew full well that those were weasel words. Drago would chop them down as soon as they showed themselves.

'Give me a rifle!' snarled Fawlkner. 'I'll give the bastard his answer.'

Del handed over a Springfield. The rancher stumbled over to the shattered window, poked the gun barrel through and launched his answer in the direction of the odious voice.

'Come and get me, Drago,' he yelled. 'The only way you're gonna get the Big Dipper is over my dead body.'

A growl of rage emerged from the cluster of trees on the far side of the corral where Drago was sheltering.

Immediately the gunfire started up again with renewed ferocity.

The defenders inside the cabin hugged the ground.

Del signalled to Lone Wolf enquiring if he was familiar with a Springfield. The boy nodded eagerly. His face assumed a rapacious gleam. Here was his chance to engage in combat. He grabbed the rifle and began returning fire through the window on the far side of the door.

The others joined him in repelling the attack.

For another half-hour the battle raged. Smoke filled the cabin, the acrid stench of burnt cordite stinging their eyes. But Del was well aware that the attackers held a distinct advantage.

There were more of them, at least ten that he had counted from the puffs of smoke launched from rifles. Not only that, they also had possession of the well. Piecrust had gone outside to refill the empty water bucket before he had been so brutally shot down.

And doubtless they had come supplied with unlimited ammunition.

The situation in which the besieged quartet now found themselves was dire.

He knew that something drastic would have to be done to swing the battle in their favour.

But what?

FIFTEEN

LEVELED!

It was Daisy who offered a solution.

She had suddenly remembered that the cabin was built over an old copper mine shaft. The ore had been worked out long before they arrived in the Anza Valley and the mine abandoned. But the level made a good escape route in the case of attack by Mexican bandits from over the border.

They had not used it for some years which is why it had been overlooked.

Del's eyes lit up. 'Where does it come out?' he asked, a nervous crack in his voice. Descending into the raw bowels of the earth did not exactly appeal. But if it was their only option, then it would have to be done.

'About one hundred yards over to the left by the rock face,' Daisy replied, moving across to the corner of the room and dragging a chest off the entrance to the shaft. Between them, she and Del heaved up the wooden trapdoor. A stink of rotting vegetation wafted up from the umbrid depths. 'We used to store vegetables down there,' she said, wrinkling her pretty nose.

Girding up his nerve, Del grabbed a hold of the prized Winchester and tentatively descended the wooden ladder. A lighted torch was clutched in his other hand.

'Wish me luck,' was his final choking remark before he disappeared into the murky gloom.

The constricted passage stank to high heaven, but it was the claustrophobic nature of the narrow passage which Del forced himself to overcome. Hemmed into the tunnel, panic threatened to consume his trembling frame. Eyes squeezed tight shut, he paused, sucking in a breath of fetid damp air and allowing his jangled nerves to settle.

Then he moved off. The tunnel had been cut through solid rock and was barely more than five feet high. Bent low to avoid cracking his head on the roof, he pressed onward willing the end of his torment to arrive.

It seemed to go on forever. One hundred yards felt more like as many miles. The ten minutes it took to cover the short distance was more like ten hours. Finally, sweat pouring down his stubbled cheeks, he espied a chink of daylight in the distance.

Quickly, the tunnel rat stumbled gratefully towards the opening at the far end. Emerging into the light of day, he had never before in his life been so relieved to suck in pure wholesome air.

But there was no time to restore his frazzled composure. The gunfire from the attackers had risen to a new level of frenzied hostility. From this new position, Del could observe the attackers moving in, dodging between the various places affording cover.

Soon they would be close enough to make a final assault. Or even set fire to the ranch house. It would be like Drago to exact the same revenge to which his properties had been subjected.

The defenders could not hold out for much longer.

Compressed eyes panned the killing ground searching for the repugnant perpetrator.

Then he saw him. Drago was hiding behind a wagon on the far side of the corral. Set back from the action so as not to place himself in any danger, the cowardly skunk was directing operations. Urging his men forward with bribes of larger bonuses, he loosed off the occasional spate of gunfire.

From where he had emerged out of the old mining level, Del could see that he was no better off than before. There was no chance of getting close to the Southern Cross tyrant without revealing himself. And with so many guns out there, he would assuredly be scythed down before he had taken a dozen steps.

Tight-lipped with frustration, Del Gannon mulled over his options. He had to do something. And quickly as well if his comrades were to be saved.

Then he remembered that he had the rifle. The *One-in-a-Thousand!* An ordinary carbine did not have the range for such an accurate shot. But the Special was a different matter.

Admittedly, Drago was probably skulking at the extreme end of its range. Del knew that he would only be allowed one shot. Miss, and the guy would be warned and thus put himself in a safe situation. The element of surprise would be lost, and he would likewise then come under attack.

At that moment, most of the target's body was concealed behind the wagon. Only his head was visible. It would need a perfect shot to take him out. Del cursed under his breath, willing the varmint to expose himself further. 'Come on, you durned bastard,' he muttered under his breath. 'Shift yer ass.'

Then it happened.

Drago shifted to his right around one side of the wagon to get a better view of the action. All his upper body was now exposed.

The sharp-shooter's eyes glinted in anticipation. The rifle settled comfortably in his right shoulder. Resting his arms on a rock, he took careful aim along the barrel. Drago was gesticulating to some of his men. The shooter sucked in a breath of air and held it. The gunsights were alligned. His finger tightened on the trigger, the knuckles blanching as the pressure mounted. A single firm tug, and gun bucked into his shoulder.

The deep-throated roar went unnoticed by the shooter whose narrowed eye followed the lead projectile towards its destination.

Still he held his breath. Only when the target keeled over and lay still did he exhale, gasping in more air as the tension in his strained muscles suddenly eased. Anxious eyes focused on to the fallen victim to ensure that he was dead.

No movement could be detected. Jackson Drago had indeed gone down to stir the Devil's cauldron.

But what of his men? Would they still continue the battle?

His orders suddenly chopped off, one of the attackers closest to his boss could see that he had been killed. That changed everything. With the source of their pay and bonuses removed, there was no longer any reason for them to stick around.

'Drago's been hit!' shouted the observer.

'Is he dead?' another asked keeping his head down.

'Sure looks that way,' was the stuttered reply.

A brief lull in the shooting followed as the import of this revelation bit home. Men looked at one another. They all realized what that meant.

'In that case, I'm gettin' out,' shouted one man slithering backwards from the line of fire to where the horses were tethered.

'Me too,' came another panicky voice. 'Ain't no sense in hangin' around to get shot at for nothin'.'

Del launched a couple more shots at the retreating cowpokes. His intention was to encourage them into vacating the battlefield in double quick time. There had been enough killing already. Only if they had chosen to carry on the fight would his gun have spoken in anger again.

In less than five minutes the attackers had vanished.

The sound of pounding hoofs faded into the distance. And if they had any sense, all of them would quit the territory. Only the body of Jackson Drago remained behind. A pair of buzzards circled overhead eager to get to grips with the tasty treat.

Slowly scrambling to his feet, Del came out from behind the cluster of rocks and approached the ranch. His rifle was held at the ready, just in case any wounded critters remained. Two bodies lay unmoving in the corral, in addition to that of Piecrust Pete.

Halfway across, the door of the cabin opened and the defenders emerged. Their faces were smoke-blackened, shoulders slumped. It was a victory for honesty and right. But too many people had died unnecessarily. Piecrust and Johnny Concho, not to mention Juan Carlos and the reformed foreman of the Southern Cross, Isaac Hayes.

The bad guys didn't count, but they were still human.

Daisy ran across to the tall Texan and threw her arms around his lean frame. It felt good. He hugged her warmly in return.

'You figure there might be a need for some extra help around here now that poor old Piecrust has gone to that cookhouse in the sky?' he asked gingerly.

'You try leaving, mister,' the girl sighed, and there'll be trouble.'

'Don't fret none,' Del assured her. 'Guess I'll buy all the oranges I need from a store, rather than grow them.'

AUTHOR'S NOTE

The legend of Pegleg Smith is no figment of the imagination. The wily character certainly lived. And the events depicted concerning his discovery are essentially regarded as being authentic. Proof of this are the samples of Black Gold that have been unearthed at frequent intervals over the years.

And even today, modern prospectors are still searching for the elusive source of the paydirt. So far without much success.

Perhaps you will have more luck. Black Gold is out there in the California Desert, just waiting for some enterprising adventurer to dig it up.